Damned if I know

<u>AS PIPPA LANGHORN</u>
Love to Hate You
Heat of the Moment

<u>AS ELIZABETH STEVENS</u>
the Trouble with Hate is…
Being Not Good
Popped
the Art of Breaking Up

Accidentally Perfect Books
Accidentally Perfect
Perfectly Accidental

Royal Misadventures
Now Presenting
Lady in Training
Three of a Kind
Some Proposal
Royally Unprepared
Royals in Dating

AVAILABLE ON WATTPAD
Austen Reimagined
Pride
Prejudice

the Danu Cycle
Gryffynhall
Elfhaven

the Damned Trilogy: Book 3

Damned if I know

ELIZABETH STEVENS WRITING AS
SCARLETT KNOX

Kinky Siren, an imprint of Sleeping Dragon Books

Damned if I know
by Scarlett Knox

Print ISBN: 978-1925928259
Digital ISBN: 978-1925928242

Cover art by: Izzie Duffield

Worldwide Electronic & Digital Rights
Worldwide English Language Print Rights

For Benjamin

Contents

One: Drake 1
Two: Wren 13
Three: Drake 26
Four: Wren 38
Five: Drake.. 51
Six: Wren 61
Seven: Drake... 73
Eight: Wren... 84
Nine: Drake 95
Ten: Wren 104
Eleven: Drake 113
Twelve: Wren 121
Thirteen: Drake... 130
Fourteen: Wren 136
Fifteen: Drake 143
Sixteen: Wren 150
Seventeen: Drake 157
Eighteen: Wren 164
Nineteen: Drake 170
Twenty: Wren 176
Twenty-One: Drake.. 181
Damned if I know... 186
Thanks 187
My Books 188
About the Author... 189

Drake

For a guy who'd never thought he'd ever get married, there was something quite surreal about finding myself married something like three times over now. A least, it was to the same woman.

The same incredible, brave, sexy, albeit fragile woman.

Wren was everything I never knew I needed or wanted. And I was sorely tempted to thank Grandad that she'd literally walked through Hell and decided to stick it out with me. I could think of nothing that scared me now.

We spent a blissful two-week honeymoon in the Caribbean – somewhat clichéd but, as soon as Wren had heard 'private island', there was very little I could do to dissuade her. And the way her face lit up in excitement, I didn't really try very hard.

Truman, Ignacio and Kyle had come along with us under the pretence of playing servants.

In reality, only Truman really fulfilled his purpose, and that was when he wasn't lounging on a beach chair with a thick book and a mojito.

Ignacio made it his mission to keep the surrounding sea shark-free. Until he decided he wanted a shark friend, then he stopped fighting them and went about trying to catch one. They were crafty though, and particularly wary after he'd gone around punching them in the nose.

And Kyle spent his time as only Kyle could. He built sandcastles. He went snorkelling. He waded in rock pools and played with sea creatures. He danced in a waterfall. And he collected about a hundred shells a day for Wren.

But the boys being distracted had suited Wren and I just fine. When we weren't strolling along forest paths or along the incoming tide at sunset, we were in bed.

For the first time in millennia, a part of me craved a normal life – a human life. I had a taste of it with her and I knew what I was missing out on. But my wife was truly Lucifer's daughter-in-law and she was happy to go home after our two weeks were up.

And if I couldn't live on Earth, then I'd bring a piece of Earth to Hell for my wife. And I'd done so in the shape of a house. It was nothing like Dad had had in mind when I first mentioned it to him. I'd managed to persuade him to make it something a little less ostentatious. Not that it was all that hard.

It seemed, when it came to my wife, my father was a bit of a soft touch.

So, we had a modest home sitting in the middle of Hell. It was the sort of thing that Wren could feel comfortable hosting her human friends and family in.

The first time she saw it was the most rewarding.

We'd just walked back into Hell, through one of the many back doors I enjoyed as a perk of my birth. I took her through the many winding corridors, nodding a curt greeting to anyone who acknowledged us. Finally, we came to the relatively out of the way tunnel between Cerberus' domain and the Unicorn Fields – save me if I wanted to make sure my wife had some extra protection close by and something nice to look at.

"What is this?" she asked with a smile as we paused outside.

From the front, it didn't look like much, granted. Unlike our previous room, it was more than just a door. It was a grand front door, windows and a balcony essentially carved into the wall of the tunnel. If that was how things worked in Hell. On the inside, it was so much more.

"This is our new home," I told her.

Kyle squeaked in excitement and ran to one of the windows, his snorkel smushed against it to see inside.

Wren took my hand and I looked at her to find her smiling. "Our new home?"

I nodded. "Yes. I thought you'd probably want more than just a bedroom. If Harmony or your family came to visit for example, you'd probably want somewhere they'd," I cleared my throat, "feel more comfortable."

"So, you got me a house?"

"I…organised a house. My father will want all the credit for the actually procuring, no doubt."

"Can we go in?" she asked and I could see by the look in her eyes that she was happy.

"Of course."

"Kyle first!" he called as he ran to the door and wrenched it open.

Ignacio hurried in behind him, carrying his comically large shark with its fishbowl over its head to let it breath.

"Shall I put the kettle on?" Truman asked us as he walked to the door with us.

"That would be lovely, Truman. Thank you," Wren said as she squeezed my hand.

At the threshold, I swung her into my arms and carried her across.

"How very romantic of you," she teased as her arms went around my neck.

"I call it protecting you from worrisome demons who might be lurking about our new home." I planted a quick kiss on her lips.

She laughed. "I don't think you have to worry about Kyle or Ignacio."

"You assume they're the only demons I'm concerned about."

"You're the prince of Hell, what demon would possibly be stupid enough to be in your home?" she asked me.

I conceded that one. The only kind I'd worry about were the charred winged kind, and it would take a very bold arsehole to not only enter my father's realm, but my own house. That was providing he made it past Cerberus, of course.

I let her down and didn't take my arm from her waist as she looked around the house, such as it was.

Downstairs was split into formal and casual living and dining areas. There was a kitchen – although no one expected any of us to use it – and a bathroom – again not strictly necessary, but I anticipated it would make Wren feel more comfortable to have one. Plus, I quite enjoyed our joint showers.

"This is so nice," she breathed happily.

"You like it?"

She nodded. "I love it."

"I love you," I told her as I pulled her towards me.

I felt her smile against my lips. "I love you."

"Come see upstairs. Kyle has his own bed!" he said and we looked up to see him halfway up the stairs.

Wren took my hand and we followed Kyle up.

I took a cursory look around for Ignacio but didn't see him or his shark.

Upstairs consisted of four bedrooms – why, I don't know – and two bathrooms – one off the main bedroom. There were windows even where it should be looking out into nothing but russet stone wall. But, through the magic of Hell, there were different scenes outside each one. There was a forest, a beach, rolling hills, and even an underwater one.

Wren wrapped her arms around my neck. "And which room's ours?" she practically purred as she pressed her body into mine.

I picked her up and her legs went around my waist automatically. As I kissed her, I walked her to our room.

"See. Kyle's bed!" he said proudly.

Wren pulled away to turn her head and see where he was. I followed her gaze and found him sitting on a miniature bed at the foot of ours. It was complete with a pillow and a Disney Princess duvet cover. He was sitting on it proudly, still wearing his snorkel and mask.

"That's a nice bed you've got there, Kyle," Wren said.

He bounced on it. "Perfect," he sighed happily.

Wren turned back to me with a big smile. "Well, someone's comfortable."

I stretched my neck and took a deep breath. "We might need to get him his own room," I said quietly.

Wren laughed and hugged me close. Her lips found mine before I'd had time to think about it and I held her tightly. Just as I took a step towards the bed, there was a very familiar voice from behind me.

"Uh, sir. Your father will be ready for you soon."

With an audible grunt of annoyance, I gently dropped Wren to her feet and turned to look at Neville.

"Come in, Neville. Make yourself at home."

He grinned his gap-toothed grin. "Thank you, sir. But I do have places to be. I am only tasked with informing you that his devilness is almost ready to welcome you home."

"Almost ready as in…?" Wren started.

"As in if you dawdle, he will be ready for you."

Wren and I exchanged a look and I didn't have to read her mind to know she was thinking the same thing as me; my father was never behind schedule. He should have been ready now. He should have been waiting for us. If he was at his happiest performing for an audience, he was at his second happiest when he was waiting on an audience.

"Great," I said to Neville. "We'll be along shortly."

He gave as low a bow as his rotund body and lack of waist would let him, then scurried out.

I wasn't even concerned about the lack of privacy we obviously had in the house just then. I was more concerned about what was going on with my father.

"We're not going to dawdle, are we?" Wren asked.

I shook my head. "No."

She nodded and I took a moment to really appreciate this human. She was braver than I could even fathom – being immortal and virtually unkillable gave you a rather superficial sense of true bravery – and she had fully accepted and immersed herself into my world. For me. I wanted to say I wasn't worth it, but I didn't want to risk her changing her mind.

"I'm all in this," she said softly, cupping my cheek.

"What?" I asked, leaning into her hand.

"I'm not going anywhere. No matter what."

She must have guessed what I was thinking by the look on my face. I gave her a quick kiss.

"Me either," I said.

"Good. Then let's go see what's wrong together."

We hurried down the stairs. Ignacio was waiting for us at the front door. Sans shark.

I paused for a moment, wondering if it was worth asking him what he'd done with it.

"She's safe," he grunted as though he knew what I was thinking and I felt like it was going around suddenly. "I made her a tank."

I decided not to ask him to elaborate and reminded myself we were back in Hell. Things just were down here.

Kyle was still snuggled in bed and Truman was probably reading a magazine and drinking a mojito, but Ignacio came with us.

Wren and I walked into Dad's throne room and saw he was leaning on his tactics table. His brow was furrowed and he wore the simplest, most boring suit pants and shirt combination.

Next to him was Mammon, who was a fearsome sight wherever you beheld him and whoever you were. In Hell, his flaming crown just sat directly upon his dark wavy hair. He, like my father, wore a suit and a scowl.

Something wasn't right.

"Yes, Mammon," my father huffed. "I'm sure we'll work it all out. It's not the first time this has happened."

Mammon nodded.

"Perhaps not. But we should–"

Dad looked up and saw us. "There are my two favourite love-birds!"

Even for him, the joviality was forced.

"What's wrong?" Wren asked, obviously noticing as well.

Dad's smile was strained. "Wrong? Why would anything be wrong, daughter?" he asked.

I frowned. "What is it?"

"Would you believe me if I told you there was a problem with the catering tonight?" Dad tried.

"No," both Wren and I said.

Dad sighed dramatically and waved his hand. "Fine. There seems to have been…" He paused, "a slight implication – shall we say – to our little trip to Earth." He flicked his hair back. "Nothing unmanageable or unexpected."

"What kind of implication?" I asked.

"The embargo kind," Mammon said and Dad threw him a dirty look like he was telling all the pinky-sworn secrets.

"Embargo?" Wren said.

Mammon nodded. "All of Earth is restricted to necessary beings. No one goes up without authorisation from Michael himself."

I looked at Dad, my eyebrow raised in question.

Dad huffed and nodded. "Yes. It's not great."

"Not great?" I exclaimed. "He doesn't get involved unless it's really bad."

"Or he's bored."

"He's not bored," Mammon and I both said.

Dad waved his hand. "Regardless. We don't need to worry ourselves about that. We've got two souls back where they belong and it's time to celebrate! Leave Michael to his clean up."

I sighed. "Clean up?"

"Irrelevant!" Dad cried happily, but I could see it didn't reach the depths of his eyes.

He might not have been able to lie, it might have been irrelevant to the fact he wanted to forget it was happening, but that didn't mean that he wasn't worried about it all the same.

I might not have known why he was worried, but I knew enough about him to be worried myself. It was the unplaced worry eating away at me that had me realising that something was already bothering me. I had the beginnings of that foreboding feeling in my stomach. My fingers were suddenly restless, calmed only by taking Wren's hand in mine.

Something definitely wasn't right. Something was coming.

I looked at my father and I knew he knew it as well. I don't know if he read my mind, but I was pretty sure neither of us knew what we were supposed to be worrying about. But we were both going to do whatever it took to not worry anyone else.

So, I let him get on with his party.

We were welcomed back to Hell, the prince and heir and his human princess, with all the fanfare I'd expected from my father.

Persephone and Esther were in attendance. As were a few of my half-brothers, two of Persephone's 'secret' lovers, and a whole host of demons in various forms.

There was dinner and a lengthy show – with an appearance from the resident juggling unicycle-riding guard demon. There were puppets dancing – Dad's favourite – and forced laughter. On the surface, everything looked fine. But underneath, the ripples of change nagged.

I realised that, from the moment we'd stepped foot through the gate, things felt different – maybe bad different, maybe not bad different – as we went about creating some sort of normal life. It wasn't just the portent-y feeling in me. It was Wren as well.

She seemed more relaxed somehow. Like she was truly home and hadn't in fact been dragged back to Hell again. She had this confidence in herself that fucking shone from her. She was strong. She was decided. She was radiant. Had I not already been irrevocably in love with her and bound to her until the end days, then that would have done it.

For most of that first night home, she didn't seem to notice anything was wrong. She just enjoyed herself. But, now and then, I noticed she'd look at me or my father as though she could tell.

She didn't say anything about it and, when we got back home, I did my best to make sure she only thought and felt happy things.

Wren

Being back in Hell really did feel like a homecoming. As much as I was sure it seemed hotter than it had last time, it felt right. Hell felt like the place I was supposed to be.

With Drake back on the job, it was up to me to find something that could be my new normal. I wasn't just down here passing the time anymore and I didn't have exams to study for. So, I needed something to occupy my time while Drake was off torturing souls.

While I looked for it, I spent the next week making our house a proper home. Which involved me mainly just wandering around and uselessly moving things to different places in the house, and just generally getting used to it as my house.

But, when I finally really got stuck into it, the first on the list was a special present for Kyle. He'd been devastated when he realised that Ignacio had a pet. He hadn't said anything outright, but I could tell that he wanted one of his own. And he had been very good to me since Drake first brought me to Hell.

I had no idea what would make an appropriate pet for Kyle. But Truman, as always, was willing to help.

"Did you want to get him something Hellborn or Earthborn, ma'am?" he asked me, mojito in claw.

"What's better?"

Truman swished his drink as he thought about it. "Hellborn would be…somewhat hardier perhaps, ma'am."

I nodded, thinking I knew where he was going with that. "Earthborn would – say, just as an example – only survive being eaten once?" I clarified.

"Indeed, ma'am."

"Okay. Well, I guess that's a pretty easy decision. So now all I need to know is if there are any Hellborn cat-like things."

"Things, ma'am?"

"Creatures. Beings. Monsters. Whatever your preference for term is, that."

He gave me a slightly sassy glance. "I can think of a few."

"Any that would suit Kyle?"

"There is the Cat Sith. A soul stealer."

"Would it then release the souls into the house much like an Earthborn cat with a bird?" I asked.

Truman inclined his head. "It's been known to happen."

"Not that then."

"The Kasha steals corpses…which is not much better?" Truman looked at me like he was checking.

I rolled my eyes. "Worse. That would be worse."

Truman nodded. "Extrapolating, that would leave the mandagot, ma'am."

"Mandagot?"

"Indeed."

"And what is a mandagot?"

"It is a great black cat-like creature. Mortals call them evil, though they're usually quite tame by Hellspawn standards. Not known for anything inherently, although some believe them to be good guards. They originate in France, but I've learnt not to hold that against them."

I thought about it. Kyle had a thing for cats. By all accounts – well, Truman's – a mandagot would survive Kyle and his accident-prone, 'taste first ask questions later' attitude.

"Okay. And where do I find a…mandagot?" I asked.

"So, you do choose a mandagot for Kyle?" Truman asked.

"Yes. I think it's probably the best I'm going to get."

Truman's now-empty glass disappeared. "I will fetch one for you, ma'am. They're usually relatively tameable. Though, we may need to give it extra lessons–"

"Kyle certainly won't," I finished for him.

"Indeed, ma'am."

"I don't suppose there are obedience classes for mandagots?" I hedged.

"From what you've learnt of Hell to date, ma'am, what do you think?"

"I think less discipline is considered the better."

"Indeed, ma'am. I'll return shortly with Kyle's mandagot."

"Thank you, Truman."

"Of course, ma'am."

He disappeared and I had to think of my next problem. What to get Truman. True, he seemed much happier since he'd discovered mojitos. Or at least, more content. But it was still pottering around Mum and Dad's that he'd been at his most content.

"Yes," I breathed, thinking about it.

What was the one thing that Truman had absolutely adored when we were on Earth?

"Gardening."

Although, how I was going to get him a garden would be an entirely different matter. I knew just the devil to help me though.

"Lucifer?" I called.

After a heartbeat, he stood in front of me. "You rang, daughter?" he said suavely.

I nodded. "Is it possible to build a garden?"

Lucifer looked around like I was mad. "A garden?"

"Yes."

"As in for flowers?"

"And vegetables. And trees. And whatever else."

"A garden. In Hell?"

I nodded again. "Yes. Is it possible?"

"Of course, it's possible, Wren."

I was taken aback. "Then why are you acting so…surprised?"

"I'm just trying to work out what my daughter-in-law could *possibly* want with a garden. You can have anything you want at the drop of a hat." To emphasise his words, he conjured and subsequently dropped a hat on the floor.

"It's not for me. It's for Truman."

Lucifer's eyes narrowed, but I wasn't sure if it was confusion or suspicion. "For Truman?"

"He really enjoyed gardening on Earth. I thought he might like to have his own little garden here. Something for him to potter about in–"

"I presume he'll mainly be growing mint for his mojitos?" Lucifer grinned.

I smiled. "I'd be perfectly happy to leave it up to him to choose what he wanted to grow. Too bad there isn't a rum tree."

"Oh, we can make one," Lucifer said absently as he looked out the front window. Or, what I'd taken to calling the front window. He ran his hand over his beard. "I don't see why not. It's a little unorthodox to have something in Hell for pleasure, but we're nothing if not good at stretching the rules. Yes. We can build Truman a garden. Where were you thinking?"

"Where would work?"

"We can put it at the side of the house. Open a cavern up." Lucifer looked up as though he could see all the rock above us. "Could add some grass, a nice patio. Would be lovely for summer barbeques." He looked back to me. "What do you think?"

I nodded. "I think it sounds good."

"Excellent."

A set of French doors appeared in the wall to my left. Lucifer walked towards them and threw them open to reveal a big open lawn. It seemed to stretch forever to the left, but ended in a lovely little picket fence in line with the front of the house to the right.

"Now. Let's get designing." Lucifer clapped his hands together in pure glee.

We spent the rest of the day together, designing – and redesigning – the garden. Mostly it was the sort of things you saw in gardens on Earth. Occasionally, Lucifer suggested something a little more suited to Hell.

He conjured up some bubbling blood pools, a few tormented souls either strung up as scarecrows or in place of statues. After the initial shock, I started just looking at him pointedly. To which he'd shrug with a look of 'oh well, I tried' and make it disappear again.

By the time Truman was back again, we were done.

We'd kept a lot of the lawn. Lucifer had insisted that we have a small forest at the edge of it and I hadn't seen the harm in it. There were raised garden beds and trees of the fruiting and general shading varieties. There was a comfortable little patio with a table and chairs to sit and drink wine with family and friends.

In one giant tree, there was also a treehouse which, according to Lucifer, was just in case Drake and I decided to get around to having our own little bundles of evil. He wasn't even fussed if it was in the form of pets or grandchildren, the offer was there.

"Ma'am?" Truman said.

I turned to see him and smiled widely at the look of confused irritation on his face.

"What have you done?" he continued.

"We made you a garden," I said proudly.

Truman blinked and looked up at me. "A garden?"

"For you," Lucifer said.

"What for?"

I spread my arms wide. "For whatever you want to do. You can grow fruits and veggies and flowers. Or just sit in the shade and read—"

"With your mojito," Lucifer added. "I even created a rum tree for you. Very proud of that one."

Truman looked out over the garden and I wasn't sure, but it looked like his eyes had become a little glassy. "But why, ma'am?" he asked.

"Because of everything you do for us, Truman. And if Drake's made me a home here, I wanted you to have one too. I saw how much you liked pottering around with Mum on Earth. So, this was the best I could do."

Sure, the 'sky' was still the roof of the cavern and I wasn't sure that we'd experience all the four seasons, but it did feel less like we were standing in the bowels of Hell.

"Ma'am, it's lovely. I don't know how to thank you. And you, sir," he said to Lucifer.

My father-in-law inclined his head. "You know I'm loathe to deny Wren any request, Truman."

"Oh!" I said, suddenly remembering. "Did you find the mandag–"

A crashing tinkle came from inside and Truman nodded.

"I suspect that was it, ma'am."

"You left it inside?"

"A mandagot?" Lucifer asked and Truman nodded again.

"Indeed, sir."

"Why in all the circles did you want a mandagot?" Lucifer asked me.

"It's for Kyle," I explained.

Lucifer went from shocked and potentially concerned to understanding. "Ah. Excellent choice. He'll love it." He gave a single nod and looked around. "Right. If my work is done for now, I have souls to torture. Wren dear, we'll see you and Drake for dinner?"

I nodded. "You will."

"Excellent. Have an infernal day."

"You too."

Lucifer faded from view. The last thing to disappear was his smile, just like the Cheshire Cat.

"Do you like it?" I asked Truman, indicating the garden.

He gave a short nod. "I do, ma'am. It was very kind of you."

I shrugged. "Not at all."

Ignacio wandered out and looked around suspiciously like he was scouring for dangers and expected them to hide behind every tree or blade of grass.

"There's a mandagot breaking things," Ignacio said, matter-of-fact.

"Don't worry about the mandagot. Have you cleaned the shark tank?" Truman asked Ignacio.

Ignacio's response was a muttered grumble that was well recognisable as a 'no and I don't want to'.

"You're the one who wanted a pet shark," Truman reminded him.

"I cleaned it last week," Ignacio grunted.

"Yes. And you need to clean it weekly. That was the deal."

"How about you clean the tank and then we go and see if Cadriel will let you play with the weapons?" I asked.

Truman and Ignacio both turned to look at me quickly. Their mouths dropped open.

"I'd mention something about catching flies here, but I haven't seen any outside the fields," I said with a smile.

"Uh, ma'am?" Truman said slowly.

"Yeah, Truman?" I answered, equally slowly.

"Have you been studying Hellspeak?"

I frowned. "No, why?"

Truman and Ignacio shared a glance. There was another tinkling crash from inside, but neither of them paid any notice to it.

"You're…" Truman cleared his throat. "You're speaking Hellspeak, ma'am."

"Have I never done that?"

Truman shook his head. "No, ma'am. To date, you've been able to understand it but you've never spoken it."

I laughed at the absurdity. But neither Truman or Ignacio were laughing. Ignacio just nodded and Truman clasped his claws in front of his body as he looked at me. My laughter died awkwardly.

"Is that…is that bad?" I asked them.

Ignacio shrugged as Truman took a deep breath and said, "It may just be you're home after all, ma'am. In tune with the…magic of Hell, so to speak."

I nodded. "Of course. That makes sense. Right?"

Truman nodded his head once. It was somehow a very loud action. "I'm sure, ma'am."

I looked to Ignacio again who just shrugged again.

"Go to see the winged git in half an hour?" Ignacio asked, already over whatever had just happened.

"If it's going to take you half an hour to clean the shark tank, then yes." I nodded.

"Okay, boss-lady."

Ignacio shuffled inside. I stood outside with Truman for a moment longer. But he seemed uneasy.

"I'll pop the kettle on, ma'am," he said before hurrying inside himself.

So, I'd spoken Hellspeak. It surely didn't mean anything more than I belonged in Hell. I was sure that was all it could be, even though there was this niggling little feeling at the back of my neck that made me feel uneasy. I didn't feel like it was a sign the world was going to end – not anytime soon at least – or something awful was going to happen. I just felt like there was something going on that I didn't understand.

I was thankfully distracted by a cup of tea, but that was short-lived as the mandagot batted it off the table as it stared at me like it dared me to do anything about it.

"Seriously?" I asked it and I could have sworn the giant black cat grinned at me.

As I opened my mouth to reprimand it, Kyle came skidding in the door, his snorkel and mask still on his face.

The room froze as Kyle eyed off the mandagot and it eyed him off. I wasn't sure who was prey and who was predator.

Then Kyle yelled, "Kitty!" and threw himself at it.

The mandagot's ears lay flat against its head and its tail swished slowly and uncertainly as Kyle hugged it around the neck. It looked at me like it thought I'd be able to do anything about it.

"Mandagot, meet Kyle. Kyle, this is your mandagot,' I said.

I was sure the mandagot frowned at me, but Kyle turned his head with a huge grin on his little red, leathery face.

"Kyle's?" he asked cautiously.

I nodded. "This mandagot is your pet now, Kyle. That means you have to look after it. Do you understand?"

Kyle nodded so fast his bat ears flapped wildly, hitting the mandagot in the face. "Take care of Kitty. Promise."

I smiled. "Good. Now–"

The mandagot was obviously done with hugs because, in one smooth movement, it pulled itself from Kyle's arms and swallowed him whole.

I blinked at it, not sure where to start. The smug look on its face seemed like a decent place, but checking on Kyle was probably better.

"Kyle?" I asked hesitantly, leaning towards the mandagot.

"Kyle okay," I heard a muffled call from the big cat's stomach.

I nodded. "Uh. All right then."

I'd heard the stories about how Cerberus had eaten Kyle on numerous occasions and it was pretty clear he'd 'survived' those. So, I was almost certain he'd survive this one.

I cleared my throat. "Um. I'm just going to leave you guys to it…"

The mandagot licked its lips and I hurried out to see how Truman was doing in the garden.

Drake

It wasn't the first time I'd wanted to stay in bed with my wife and I knew it wouldn't be the last.

I still marvelled at the fact that I, the son of Lucifer, had fallen in love with a human. The proper kind of love where you want to spend all your time with them and just watch them smile for hours on end. As opposed to the kind where you just want to kill them and hug their entrails while you sleep.

I hugged Wren closer and dipped my nose to her neck to breathe her in. She always smelled like sunshine and warmth. Not the blazing fire of the pits of Hell warmth. The kind that gave you that settled feeling in the pit of your stomach, gave your heart a reason to beat, and felt oh so right.

If it was up to me, we'd stay in bed all day.

Wren sighed audibly. "Yeah. Well, as much as I'd like that, you've got responsibilities."

I pulled back and looked at her. "What?"

"What, what?"

"What do you mean?"

Wren turned to face me, a humoured smirk at her lips. "I mean I would also like to stay in bed all day. But alas, we can't."

I frowned as I looked her over. As much as I knew she didn't like it when I did, I dipped into her mind.

Is he okay? was the only thing in there.

I had to ask myself the same question. I'd been sure I'd thought the bit about staying in bed all day, but maybe I'd inadvertently spoken out loud.

I must have. Wren couldn't have heard it if I didn't say it out loud. Celestials – of which Nephilim were only one species – were basically the only beings I knew of who could read minds. Minus a few of the older, more unique Hellspawn, there were currently only two beings in Hell who could read minds.

"You okay?" she asked me.

I nodded, but it felt stilted. I was okay, in the strictest sense of the word. "Just didn't realise I'd spoken out loud."

She smiled up at me and lay her hand on my cheek. She drew me down to her lips. "It's not the end of the world," she said before she kissed me gently.

But it wasn't the kind of kiss that turned into makes-you-late-for-work morning sex. It was just the kind to make your heart skip a beat and your stomach flutter pleasantly.

I felt Wren smile against my lips before she pulled away. "Don't you have souls to torture?" she asked me.

I sighed and nodded. "In a monotonous never-ending, day after day, line of souls, yes."

She chuckled. "All right. Say hi to Rene for me."

I nodded as I swung myself out of bed. "Will do."

I looked back at her and groaned. She lay back against her pillows with a cheeky little smirk at her lips.

"That is hardly fair," I told her.

She sat up, keeping the covers over her chest. "I thought torture was part of the whole Hell experience?"

I shook my head as I started getting dressed. "You've adjusted far too well."

"Are you complaining? I could always sit in the corner and rock in panic for a bit if that would make you feel better?"

I snorted – all class, all dignity. "My father would say that was beneath you."

She sighed. "That he would."

Finally dressed – and having the urge to rip it all off and get back into bed with her – I went over and pressed a quick kiss to her lips. "I'll see you later."

"I'll be here."

"Love you."

"Love you, too."

I gave her a short smile, rearranged the bulge in my jeans, which made her laugh, and headed out to my work.

With Wren to come home to each night, I felt less bored as I went about my day of torturing. With the embargo on Earth, there was no collecting to be done to break up the monotony, but I found I didn't need it.

I did my inspections, Ignacio at my side and threatening to eat people alive as always. The Torture Grounds were looking as forlorn as usual. The murderous flower that had escaped the Unicorn Fields was easily herded back where it was promptly eaten by a teddy bear. The personal hells were running as smoothly as ever. The Naked for My Presentation hells were always one of my favourites.

I saw Larry and his a capella group. They all asked how Wren was doing and if Kyle had tried to eat his mandagot – or Ignacio's shark – yet.

"Bessie's safe," Ignacio told them.

"Bessie?" Larry asked.

"The shark," I told him. "The mandagot is still just Kitty."

"Good name for a mandagot, there," Larry said with a nod of his shadowy head.

"I guess it is."

"I s'pose we'd best let you get on then, Drake."

"Appreciate it, Larry. Souls won't torture themselves." I amended, "Most souls won't torture themselves."

There were plenty of personal hells where they did. There were some souls who only made it to Hell because of the weight of their guilt over something. Without it, they might not have been sent to us, but guilt could be powerful. Too much of it and you were deemed guilty of sin.

"Ah, well. Keeps you in a job, eh?"? he asked.

I nodded. "That it does."

"See you later, Drake."

"Later, Larry."

Larry and Ignacio exchanged a wave as Ignacio and I headed off for our next job.

Rene hadn't tried escaping since the Cerberus incident the day Dad had told me I was getting married. Which wasn't surprising really. Hell had only gone a couple of years while I was on Earth getting married.

"Hey, Drake," he said from his position in the stocks.

"Rene. Having an infernal day?"

"You know it."

I picked up a knife. "What do you feel like today? Judas Cradle? Catherine Wheel? Spanish Boot? Haven't used the Pear of Anguish in a while."

"Oh, how about Catherine Wheel? Ignacio can help then."

I looked at Ignacio, who rubbed his claws together and nodded. "All right. Catherine Wheel it is. You want the wheel or the saltire?"

"Saltire, why not. Mix it up a bit."

"Can do."

The stocks disappeared and Rene was lying tied to the large X.

"Ignacio, choose our weapon," I told him.

Ignacio chose his weapon with the kind of glee Cadriel felt in a human strip club. He held up the club for me.

"Simple, yet effective."

I picked on up as well and we set to work.

Through the screaming and the blood splatter, Rene and I talked about Wren and Earth – he was very interested in what it was like now. Ignacio whacked me a couple of times when he thought I was getting too distracted.

When everyone of Rene's bones were broken, I wiped the latest splatter off my face. Ignacio grinned at me widely, all of his pointy little teeth on show. You could barely see the blood against his skin, but his leg hair was matted.

"I guess we'll call it a day then," I said to Rene, looking to Ignacio for his opinion.

"Much obliged, Drake," Rene said as Ignacio nodded.

The mechanism of Hell would leave Rene to wallow in his torment for a while, then he'd be whole again and ready to go through it all again. Same as every day.

"Dinner soon, boss," Ignacio said.

There was just enough time for a shower with Wren first.

"I'll see you later, Rene."

"Later, Drake."

I patted his leg on the way out and he screamed in pain. I nodded proudly, relishing the feeling of job satisfaction that still felt new to me.

Ignacio and I headed home to clean up, I had some time with Wren, then we headed for the throne room.

We'd taken to having dinner with Dad most nights, which wasn't all that odd considering that was what I usually did when Persephone was back. Since she'd only come back once an Earth year, I hadn't seen her very often compared to the time I'd been stuck with Esther. But, thank Grandad that time worked differently because then I'd at least see Seph for a good few hundred years at a time.

I knew Wren was enjoying seeing the dynamic between my two stepmothers. Not in the least because they were almost always hostile to each other, but they were on the same side when it came to exasperation over my father's theatrics.

Case in point, Dad was currently dressed up as a musketeer and had one of the more humanoid demons dressed up as Robin Hood to settle the debate of who would win. Not that it was actually going to settle the debate because Dad would win no matter who was dressed up as who – that's just how it worked.

It was yet another excuse for my father to play dress-up and keep an audience captive, quite literally. Wren, Seph, Esther and I were the only ones in the room with the power to move, but it was so not worth it to try and save ourselves the pain of witnessing Dad's dramatics.

He was prancing back and forth with his rapier swishing while Everit pretended to 'miss' hitting him with his arrows.

"Ha ha, I have you now, you English scum!" he chuckled with an exaggerated French accent.

"Oh no," Everit said dully. "Not even the awful sheriff could stop me. But you have done it, Aramis."

I heard Wren cough and turned to see her stifling a laugh.

My gaze then wandered over to my stepmothers. Though you could feel the hate coming off them, they sat next to each other as the wives of my father were expected to do. Also despite hating each other, they were exchanging their own look of exasperation which had nothing on the one Everit was failing to hide.

Had my father not been involved, Persephone the goddess and Esther the demon queen may well have had an amicable relationship. Or at least a neutral one. But, as it was, my father was all up in their business.

Esther served as a reminder to Persephone that the world was constantly changing, and that my father was bound to change right along with it. She was also a thorn in the heart as there was – as small and ignored as it was – a small part of Seph that loved Hades and resented him for taking another wife.

Not that Esther was pleased Lucifer had another wife. Esther knew full well that Persephone would always come first in my father's heart – such as it was. Esther knew she was nothing but an obligation. There was no love lost between her and my father – Esther's heart was a cold as her blood. But she was a proud demoness and detested being second fiddle to anyone, let alone a goddess.

It's a fine line between love and hate, I thought.

"That's how I felt about you when you first brought me here," Wren said as she took my hand.

I turned to look at her in surprise. I knew I hadn't spoken out loud this time. Which made me think that she quite clearly had read my mind. Not only that day, but I wondered about the day we got back and she'd seemed to read my mind, but I'd assumed she'd just read the look on my face.

"What?" she asked, smiling happily.

I shook my head, not sure what to say. "I… Did you just read my mind?"

I caught the panic in her green eyes before she chuckled. "No. Don't be silly. I can't read minds."

"You're not *supposed* to be able to read minds," I said.

Wren wriggled in her chair and turned back to watch Dad's 'showdown'. "No. And I can't either."

I felt like there was more to it. Like she knew something else she wasn't saying. I was very tempted to dip into her mind, but I knew how she felt about that. Something was bothering her or worrying her, but that didn't really give me the excuse to invade her privacy when I knew she preferred I didn't.

Are you sure?

"Yes, I'm sure," she said testily.

I opened my mouth to set her to rights, but Dad spoke first.

"If I'm not interrupting your conversation, Drake?" he asked, hand on hip and waving his rapier in the air.

I frowned at him. "Aren't good actors supposed to ignore the crowd?" I quipped.

Dad huffed. "Like you know anything about the theatre."

I glared at him and waved my hand to tell him to get on with it. He and Everit went back to their uneven match until Everit got bored and let himself be run through with Dad's sword.

"We had a whole ten more pages rehearsed!" Dad whined as everyone was forced to clap for him.

"Oops," Everit said, quite clearly not caring.

Dad sighed exaggeratedly and, with a wave of his hand, the spectators were gone and the five of us were sitting at the dining table.

"How was your day, Wren?" Seph asked.

She smiled at her. "Fine enough. It's mainly housetraining Kitty."

"Kyle is besotted, though!" Dad said happily. "He's even teaching Kitty to play fetch."

Which was going well. For the mandagot. Kyle's version of teaching it fetch was to catapult himself across the lawn so it could fetch him. But Kyle was enjoying himself, so I wasn't going to suggest he try any other way.

Wren was pushing her food around on her plate.

"You okay?" I asked her.

She looked at me and nodded. "Fine. I was just thinking about they whole food of Hell thing."

"What about it?" Persephone asked.

Wren dropped her fork and looked at my father. "You obviously knew."

Dad's eyes widened in a terrible attempt at innocence. "Knew what?"

"That if I ate the food of Hell, then I'd be bound to it," Wren said.

Dad nodded slowly. "I did. Of course, I did. I was the one who offered Persephone the pomegranate seeds, wasn't I?"

"You mean the one who tricked me into eating pomegranate seeds of Hell and forced me to be your wife," Seph said.

Dad rolled his eyes. "Millenia. Millenia and you can't let that go."

"It was my freedom, Hades."

"And what about my freedom?" Wren asked.

Dad shrugged. "Well, I didn't want the knowledge – or reminder in Drake's case – to get in the way of the timeline."

"Timeline?" I asked.

Dad nodded. "I knew how this was going to end. True love. Wedding bells. Passionate sex. The setback if I reminded everyone about the whole mortal eating in Hell thing seemed so not worth it."

"You did not know how it was going to end," I said incredulously. "You know a fuck tonne, but you're no prophet."

Dad sighed. "Fine. I didn't know all the details. But I *hoped* you'd fall in love and thus it wouldn't be a problem."

"That was a pretty big gamble," Wren said.

"Not at all. If he failed the first time, he'd have every year when you came back to give it another shot." Dad grinned.

"All because you wanted me to fall in love? Why?"

"Because romance is romantic. And the human in you deserved a little something more than…" He waved his hand around, indicating all of Hell, "this, son."

"You're playing the caring father card?"

"I play the cards I hold, Drake." His tone suggested he was apologetic, but I highly doubted it.

I frowned at him. "Sure you do."

"Come now," Seph said brightly. "Let us be thankful things worked out and it wasn't a problem."

"Exactly," Dad said. "Serenity is the first mortal daughter of Hell and she wears that title oh so well."

I looked at Wren and she smiled. She certainly didn't seem to think there was a problem. She looked proud of my father's words. She looked proud to be a daughter of Hell. I wasn't a praying man, but I was indeed thankful for the mercies that brought me my wife.

Wren

The rhythmic hum of Hell felt stronger than it had when Kyle and I used to lie on the floor and feel in deep in our bones. And I didn't even have to lie on the floor to feel it.

The strength of my awareness of it ebbed and flowed. Sometimes it was the background music to my day. Other times, I had to focus on it to notice it was still in fact keening away in the back of my mind.

Both felt completely normal, but combined with the fact that Truman had told me I'd spoken Hellspeak and Drake had said I'd read his mind, I didn't know what was happening to me. Was I becoming something other than human? And was that a good or bad thing?

Visions of me being a horrible Hellbeast ran through my mind. And I'd seen plenty of them to give me enough material. There were humanoid demons – much like Esther, Pen and Everit – who were shaped like humans but wrong somehow.

Some were like Esther and just not a colour you'd find among humanity – white as snow, blue, bright orange, flame red, yellow as the sun. There was always something else inhuman about them. It could have been their eyes. It could have been leathery wings or horns or hooves. It could have been an extra limb, or an eye or razor-toothed mouth in the middle of their stomach. It might have even just been elongated limbs with claws at the ends, all the better for slashing with.

Other demons were definitely inhuman. There were, of course, the devilbums, the rolly-polly guard demons, the shades – like Larry – but there were also numerous other grotesque kinds of demons I'd had trouble keeping up with.

Some were serpent like, with or without arms, and most often travelled around in multiples of twos. Others were great big skeletons made of a mish-mash of bones that ambled along the tunnels slowly. There were winged, screeching creatures that liked to duck low and skim their talons through your hair as they passed. There were creatures made of shadows that, when they fell over you chilled the blood in your veins and made you feel ill.

At that was just the tip of the iceberg. No matter how many creatures I met, questions I asked, or books I read, I didn't think even the rest of time was going to be enough for me to know about them all, let alone name them.

Needless to say, while I wasn't sure how many and what kind of demons used to be humans – other than the shades – but I was easily able to imagine myself becoming any of them. My apparent favourite daymare was me turning into one of the Pontianak and having to fight a wendigo on Tussle Tuesdays for the whole of Hell's amusement.

I didn't feel like that was likely to happen and the idea seemed so far-fetched that I wasn't concerned about it. But I kept thinking about it.

Because, surely, me changing meant something and I was having a hard time telling myself that it was just me belonging in Hell. I was still human, after all. An alive human. Alive humans didn't gain the ability to read minds, speak Hellspeak or tune into the hum of Hell without making a pact with the devil – that much I knew.

But there was little I could do about it and, since I wasn't panicking about it, I figured the best thing to do was continue on with my life. Which meant finding me a job, of sorts. Drake had mentioned there'd be something I could do down there to occupy my time, so I was going to find it.

Not really knowing what there was, I knew there was one being who'd be able to help me out. So, I was walking to the throne room when I came across Persephone in the tunnel.

We'd been back for a couple of weeks now, so surely winter was over on Earth.

"I thought you'd have left by now," I said to her.

"You that eager to get rid of me?" she joked.

"Not at all. I was just curious about the whole time thing."

She looked like she had a secret. "As you humans say, spring has sprung in the northern hemisphere."

"And you didn't take the first opportunity to leave?" I asked, surprised. I hadn't known her for long, but it didn't take a genius to see how much she didn't belong there – she belonged in open fields under the bright sunshine.

Persephone smiled back at me. "Well, it's a three-month minimum. I thought maybe I'd extend it to six-months this year and spend some time with you two."

"We'd be here next year."

Persephone shrugged. "Being a part of new beginnings is my wont," she said cryptically. "Now, tell me. What are you doing today?"

I sighed. "I'm looking for a job."

"A job?"

I nodded. "A job. Something to keep me occupied until… Is it the end days?"

Persephone smiled. "That's the one. Have you got any ideas?"

"Not really. Drake suggested a few things hypothetically, but I'm not really sure what would suit me. I mean, it would have to be in Hell, obviously. Commuting would be a bitch – these timelines make everything so confusing."

"Of course. I don't really see you as the torture kind, though."

"Probably not so much. At least, not the bloody, screaming, insides on the outsides sort."

She gave me a knowing smirk. "No. I don't blame you."

"It has been suggested I could help look after the baby devilbums…?" I wasn't sure if I was asking her or telling her.

Seph seemed to think about that for a moment. "I could see you doing quite well at such a job. It can be hard, thankless work though."

"Have you done it?"

She chuckled and it was like a Spring breeze tinkling around me. "Goodness, no. But I have dealt with baby devilbums. You think Kyle's young and naïve? He's got nothing on the real babies."

"Do you know where they are?"

She nodded. "The hatchery."

"They're hatched?"

"Not really. Sort of. Suffice to say that 'nursery' sounded a touch too…."

"Tame?" I tried.

"Tame will do."

"Will you take me to them?"

"The wife of Lucifer's son hasn't quite learned her way around Hell yet?" she teased, but I felt it was good-natured.

"Almost," I said with a smile. "I feel like I do, but I also seem to get a little lost sometimes and the boys need to come and bail me out. Ignacio barely lets me out of his sight lately."

Persephone motioned I follow her and we headed off down the tunnel. "Really? Where is he now?"

"I told him I was just coming to the throne room and he trusted me enough to go by myself. He's at home playing with his shark."

"Speaking of pets, how is Kyle enjoying his mandagot?"

I laughed. "Oh, so much. He loves it. As far as I know, he hasn't even tried to eat it yet."

"That's quite good."

"For the mandagot, yes. Less so for Kyle."

"Oh, how come?"

"It keeps eating him."

Persephone laughed. "Of course it does."

"Apparently it tickles more than when Cerberus eats him."

Persephone nodded thoughtfully. "I can well imagine."

"How does Cerberus feel about you?" I asked her, not sure what would make me say such a thing.

"He's of my time. As the queen of the underworld, he also obeys me."

"As well as he obeys your husband?" It felt weird calling him Lucifer to her when she thought of him as Hades.

She grinned, but it didn't reach her eyes. "Some would say better because he knows I won't let him get away with it. But, though he obeys me, he has no love for me."

"Why not?"

"Because he, like you, knows I don't belong here."

I swallowed, feeling guilty. "Sorry–"

"Do not be sorry," she said with a smile and a friendly nudge. "I can't read thoughts like our husbands, but I understand feelings. You know I don't belong because I'm made of the Earth. I see no malice or pity in your knowledge, only understanding. And, for that, I couldn't possibly be angry."

I smiled, but felt it prudent to change the subject. "Do you know Grace?" I asked.

"I've known a lot of Graces in my time."

"The gatekeeper."

Persephone nodded slowly. "I know Grace."

"Do you know what happened? Why she's been punished to eternity as a gatekeeper?"

"I do, but it is not my story to tell."

As much as the nosey parker in me wanted to know, I understood that.

"Here we are," Persephone said as we came to an archway. "The hatchery."

I looked inside and it looked just like any Earth daycare centre. If Earth daycare centres catered to tiny red, faun-like creatures with a propensity for destroying whatever they came into contact with.

Little devilbums ran around the room, screaming and crying. The all wore diapers and I wondered how much that had to do with them going through the motions or if that was a necessity. Lots of them were fighting with each other, swinging unwieldy axes and swords that were twice as big as them. Some were playing at executioner.

Among them all, trying to keep a modicum of control over the whole thing, were a couple of the rolly-polly demons and devilbums the size of Truman and Ignacio.

"Remind me again why Hell has a…daycare centre for devilbums?" I said to Persephone. "What even is their purpose."

"Their purpose is mayhem," she said fondly and I looked at her to see she was smiling warmly. "Pure and simple mayhem. The hatchery is here to raise them both for that purpose and to teach them not to be overly annoying to the rest of Hell. Left to their own devices, they are unmanageable and Hades was becoming sorely tempted to either just wipe them all from existence or send them to Earth to be someone else's problem."

"That's awful."

Persephone nodded as though she didn't disagree, but there was much more to it than that. "Thus, the hatchery was born.

Here, Hades feels he can…guide them to the kind of mayhem that he'll enjoy and won't annoy him."

"So, what are they learning?"

"Battle is a favourite among many of them. They also learn acting–"

"For Shakespeare Saturdays?" I interrupted.

"Among many other things Hades has tried over the eons to alleviate his boredom. They also learn torture techniques for helping in the fields. Serving. Simple letters and numbers. Languages."

"I thought they were…" What was the word Truman had used? "built to understand all languages?"

"They are but, like anything, practise helps. Do you want to go in?"

I was feeling something I could only describe as a maternal instinct. I had an urge to go in and play with these babies, to help them learn, and to watch them grow.

I nodded. "Definitely."

"My queen," one of the devilbums squeaked. "Princess."

Persephone nodded to it. "Wren and I are here to help."

"Help, ma'am?" It looked between us like it had no concept of the word.

"Yes. Wren is looking for something to occupy her time and we thought she could help out in the hatchery. Keep an eye on some of the babies, help them learn, that sort of thing."

The devilbum looked clearly frazzled but, with the amount of babies running around virtually uncontrollably, I wasn't surprised nor did I blame it.

"I don't see why not, ma'am. We could always use the extra hands. Trik, ma'am," it said holding its claw out.

I took it and shook it. "Nice to meet you."

"Trik's been working in the hatchery since it started," Persephone said. "She knows the place inside out."

Trik nodded. "The little buggers are yet to find a secret tunnel I don't already know about," she said proudly.

"That's impressive."

"That's work in the hatchery ma'am. What do you want to start with?" Trik asked.

Persephone pointed to a group who looked like they were just learning about weapons. "How about them?"

Trik's eye widened, but she nodded. "Have at it."

"Come, Wren," Persephone said.

I nodded to Trik and followed Persephone through the gambolling babies, being wary of pikes and cannon balls, and over to the little group.

"Have we just started our combat skills?" Persephone asked them, kneeling down on the floor.

They all paused in what they were doing and nodded.

"Pike," one said, holding the pike up. It had a squeakier voice than Truman, Ignacio and even Kyle. Its eyes were bigger in its head, like it needed to grow into them. And it was the same with its ears – great big droopy things that seemed far too big for it.

"I see that. Now, why don't you show us what you've learnt so far?" Persephone said to them.

The ten or so of them scrambled excitedly into two lines and faced off against each other. Then all Hell literally broke loose. Some of them bopped each other on the head. Some of them waved their sword threateningly while growling. And the one with the pike managed to poke itself before it fell on its bottom.

"Oh, no," Persephone said gently as she called one over. She lay her hand over its claw on the sword. "You've got to really stab them, sweetie."

Persephone showed them in pairs how to better injure each other. While the others waited, they sat around me and cheered happily. The one with the pike crawled into my lap and fell asleep.

When she was looking for it for its turn, Persephone turned and saw it. Her smile was at once warm and encouraging as it was calculating and knowing.

"You're very good with them, dear. Once we've taught you what they need to know, I think it will be a wonderful fit."

As much as the idea of teaching babies to hurt each other – or others – felt weirdly wrong, it also felt normal And I agreed that it was something I wouldn't mind doing to occupy my time. Helping the next generation of devilbums to be sightly less annoying sounded great.

"Do you think so?" I asked, wanting her approval.

She nodded. "I really do. I think you'd be perfect for it. It would be…good practise, yes?"

I felt my cheeks flush. "Practise?"

"For the tiny pitter patter of your own Hellspawn?"

I laughed as I ran my fingers over the head of the baby in my lap. Its nose wrinkled adorably in its sleep and I felt myself smile.

"Drake and I haven't talked about kids yet."

"Maybe not. But you want them."

I nodded. "I think so. I guess they're one of those things that I seem to know I want, but don't really think about it."

"Well, we never know what the future holds, Wren. Who knows? We might get the pitter patter of new Hellspawn sooner than you think."

I smiled. "Maybe. Maybe not. I'm honestly not sure what Drake would think about it."

"I think he'd be excited to have more of you to love."

I looked at her and felt a connection with her. It was sad that she'd eventually have to leave and it would feel to me like she'd been gone forever. But then, I supposed I'd get used to it in time. After a few cycles of the Earth, I'd be used to time seeming endless in Hell and the time she was here and gone would both blur into the simple passing and stagnating of time.

At least that was how Drake had once described it. But it made sense to me.

"Well, whenever we finally have kids, I hope you'll be here to see them into the underworld."

Persephone took my hand. "I wouldn't miss it for all the riches on Earth, darling."

Drake

If Wren wasn't getting somehow stronger each day, then I was imagining things. I just couldn't pin point how she was getting stronger.

There was just this feeling in me that she was getting stronger. It wasn't a physical strength. Not really.

She seemed happier each day. Truly happy. She'd taken up helping with the baby devilbums and it suited her well. I was also selfish enough to admit that I was glad she had something to stop her getting bored or sick of Hell and then, by extension, me.

Because I knew I'd never be bored or sick of her. And the idea she could change her mind at any time scared the Heaven out of me.

We were both getting dressed when I saw she was pulling on denim overalls.

"Where did you get those?" I asked.

"Where do I get everything?"

"Truman?"

"Truman." She looked at me. "What? You don't like them?"

I shook my head. "No. You look…adorable."

"Adorable?" she snorted. "Because it's all wives' dreams to have their husbands think they're adorable."

"I wasn't aware overalls were your new seduction outfit. Are we roleplaying now?"

"Very cute," Wren laughed and made to push me away jokingly.

Except I was obliged to step backwards from the force of it. Me, who was far stronger than her and who had been immovable against all but the most powerful of beings in all of Grandad's creation, and I'd been pushed backwards by a human.

This wasn't like those times I took a step back because I knew that's what she wanted. This was completely involuntary and it shouldn't have happened.

"Wren?" I said slowly.

"Mm?" She looked up at me in question and I wasn't quite sure what I'd been meaning to say.

"Come with me, yeah?"

Her brows furrowed in confusion. "Where are we going?"

I held my hand out for her and she took it unhesitatingly. "We need to see my father."

"Why?"

I swallowed. "Because you're changing."

Those green eyes widened. It wasn't quite panic. She did look worried, but somehow like she knew it was for the best. She didn't disagree with me and she wanted to see if there were answers.

After a pause, she nodded. "Okay."

I wasn't sure what scared me more. The fact she was facing the unknown with such calm and acceptance, or that she was obviously not exactly human anymore.

I dragged her through the tunnels to the throne room and found Dad and my stepmothers in there. Dad was at his tactical table as he often was these days. Persephone and Esther were sitting by the fire. Persephone was reading and Esther was knitting…with human entrails by the look of it.

"Dad, there's something wrong with Wren," I said.

All three of them looked up at us.

"What do you mean by wrong?" Dad asked.

"She's changing somehow. She's stronger. She shoved me."

Persephone's smile was knowing. The kind where she knew something you didn't and she was just waiting to see how long it would take you to work it out. Unlike Cadriel, she wasn't gleefully waiting for that something to bite you in the arse, but she was still looking forward to the outcome whether it was pleasant or not.

Disconcertingly, Esther was looking at me in the same way. Only I was pretty sure she was waiting for whatever it was to bite me in the arse.

"Let me get this right. You're worried because Wren managed to…shove you…?" Dad said sceptically, looking between us like it was the most ridiculous thing he'd ever heard. He leant towards me with his hand at the side of his mouth. "I don't think you need to placate her strength, son."

I huffed. "I didn't placate her. She shoved me fair and square. Hands to my chest and I stumbled."

"So, she's stronger?"

"She's also been reading my mind."

"And apparently I speak Hellspeak now?" Wren added. "Oh, and the hum of Hell is sometimes…louder. Deeper. Something like that."

Dad looked at my stepmothers then back to me. A look passed over his face I didn't understand and he started down the dais steps towards us.

"There is very little in my domain I do not know about…" he started slowly. "There is very little on Earth I cannot know if I put my mind to it. But I will admit that even I have…blind spots."

"What sort of blind spots?" Wren asked and I heard the panic in her voice.

Dad walked over to her and looked her over like he was looking for something. Suspicion marred his features as a frown furrowed his forehead.

"What are you expecting to see?" I asked, taking a step forward, but he held his hand up to stop me.

He stepped closer to her and seemed to be breathing in her scent. His eyes drew together before he pulled back quickly, staring at her pensively. His gaze darted to me, back to Wren, then over to my stepmothers.

"I suppose you knew?" he asked, pointing to Wren.

Persephone smirked. "Of course."

"And that's the real reason you stayed?"

Her smirk grew. "Of course."

Dad sighed.

"What is it?" Wren squeaked. "Am I growing horns or something? Becoming a succubus? *Can* I become a succubus?"

My father began to smile as he looked her over once more. This time, like a caress, it was soft and awed. "While it's possible for a human to become a succubus, it is impossible for you to become a succubus," he said as though that was reassuring.

Wren frowned. "Then what's the…" She petered off and her mouth dropped open into a perfect little 'o'. "No?" she breathed like she'd figured it out.

Dad nodded. "Oh, yes." He sounded incredibly proud.

"What?" I asked, panic starting to rise.

It was perfectly possible for a human to become almost any kind of Hellspawn. It took something utterly extraordinary and very rarely happened on purpose, but it was, as my father had said, possible. So, what the Heaven was my wife turning into?

I wracked my brain for all the lore.

The list of the kinds of human-born demons was extensive. Becoming one often involved murder, cannibalism or vegetarianism – depending on your culture – some gruesome hobby like pulling finger nails off for a human mosaic, or a burning need for revenge after having your heart figuratively ripped out at the root and incinerated into a trillion little pieces.

Your standard stuff.

Wren had, to my knowledge, not been involved in anything like that. The closest to a diabolical thing she'd been involved in was marrying me and that wasn't enough to get you a demonship. Damned, maybe. But no one was awarding you your horns for that.

She hadn't died, so being one of the species of ghost – spectre, wraith, poltergeist, phantom, spirit, or even soul – wasn't on the cards. Thane would have given me a head's up on that one if I'd somehow missed it.

Nothing else had a human origin.

I frowned at Persephone, trying to work it out. "You knew?"

She nodded, pressing her lips together like she was keeping mum on a secret.

"Oh, it's not Persephone who's going to be mum," Dad said, smiling widely at Wren.

It felt like my brain had shorted out. I was almost convinced I knew what he was talking about, but something in me refused to acknowledge it at the same time. I blinked, stupidly, as my eyes shifted between my wife and my father.

Finally, they dropped to Wren's stomach.

"We have a winner," Dad cried.

My eyes darted up to Wren's and I saw the joy in them. She nodded gently and I watched in slow motion as her hand went to her belly.

"Fuck," was the first word out of my mouth.

And I didn't need hindsight to know that wasn't the right thing to say.

"Really?" Dad asked incredulously. "You find out you're going to be a father and that gem of articulation is all you've got?"

I opened and closed my mouth a couple of times, but nothing wanted to come out.

Wren was smiling, though. "Give him a minute."

The way she said that – with such conviction that my real reaction wasn't only coming, but that it would be far more favourable – filled me with dread and made me feel slightly calmer all at the same time.

"Wren's pregnant?" I asked, very much asking for clarification before I could work out how I felt about that.

Persephone was the one who clapped her hands together and cried, "Yes," before she pushed herself off her chair and glided over to us.

"And you knew?" I asked her.

She gave me one of those cheeky 'guilty, but you still love me' looks and I had to admit that I wasn't really angry with her. "I *am* the goddess of new life after all."

"You're pregnant?" I looked at Wren.

My wife shrugged. "I guess so. I don't know how–"

"Did Sam and Brian never give you the birds and the bees talk, dear?" Dad asked and I rolled my eyes.

But Wren laughed. "No. They did. I'm thinking a little more mechanical than…" She frowned. "No. It makes perfect sense, really."

She caught my eye and I couldn't help catching her thoughts as well.

All that unprotected sex. With a human. Yeah. I really shouldn't have been surprised that it had ended with an impending baby.

It had been holy good though.

The corner of her lips tipped up like she knew what I was thinking. Probably because she could now. Then confusion dawned on her face.

"Hang on. What's me being pregnant got to do with me shoving Drake or…"

"Or what?" Dad pressed.

"Reading my mind," I said with a shrug.

Dad's smile was quite similar to Cadriel's except, where Cadriel was waiting for all the hurt, Dad was waiting for all the knowledge to hit.

"The kid," I said.

Dad nodded. "The kid, as you so elegantly put it, is part Nephilim. It has powers of its own. Powers that are, for lack of a better word, leaking to Wren."

"So, I'll lose them when it's born?"

"Sometimes," was all the cryptic answer we were getting out of him.

Persephone lay a hand over Wren's stomach. "My guess is about eight weeks, give or take."

"You can tell?" Wren asked.

She nodded. "Not like an exact science."

"Plus, the whole Hell timeline thing makes things a little harder," Dad added.

"But, I'm pregnant," Wren said, looking at me and smiling widely.

I nodded. "You're pregnant."

"We're going to have a baby."

"Usually how these things work," I teased.

Her smile got more rueful. "Unless it's twins, then you get two."

I looked to Persephone in panic.

"Just the one," she assured me.

I breathed out. "Just the one."

It was terrifying, surprising, exciting, and I had no idea if I was ready for it. I was just getting used to the idea I could love and be loved. Kids hadn't even got to the widest outskirts of my radar.

But, looking at my wife, I knew I wanted it. It felt right. Maybe sooner than I'd planned, but right all the same.

"Okay?" Wren asked.

I nodded. "Very okay."

"Then… Time to party!" Dad cried excitedly.

I rolled my eyes, but said nothing as glitter and confetti rained down from the ceiling, and Wren laughed happily.

Wren

So, I was pregnant.

Not surprising if you thought about how much practise Drake and I had done. I stupidly hadn't thought about the consequences. Had Drake been human, I would have. But since when did human laws, customs or consequences apply to our relationship?

When it came to biology apparently.

I'd never felt such a simultaneous combination of sheer terror and eager anticipation as I did on finding out I was pregnant.

Some days, terror won out when I remembered that my baby was part Nephilim. Who knew what even part-Nephilim babies did to their mothers?

Because I'd heard all the stories about what Nephilim babies did to their mothers. And that was if they were lucky enough to survive to term.

But mostly I was just excited.

Excited to be creating new life.

Excited to be a mum.

Excited to be growing our family, as motley as it was.

We already had humans, archangels, Nephilim, devilbums, demons, and God. After that, any baby of ours would be relatively normal.

It did, of course, mean forgoing wine at dinner – even Alexander's favourite – but it was a price I was more than willing to pay.

"It's kind of like a pact with the devil like that, huh," I said one afternoon.

"What is and how?" Drake asked.

"This whole having a baby thing."

"Is like making a deal with my father?"

I nodded. "Think about it. I'm growing a human, but there's a whole bunch of stuff I can't do now."

"No. You *could* do all that, you just won't because it's bad for the baby."

"What do you mean?"

"There are plenty of women who still drink to excess or take drugs. Losing the baby can be the best outcome for it in those situations."

I frowned at him. "What do you know about it? You were only on Earth until you were eight."

He shifted on his feet. "My aunt wasn't well. She refused to get professional help, drank too much, and decided a baby was what she was missing. Well, she got two. Then killed the third by drinking too much. Still didn't fix her. Fucking surprise."

"I'm so sorry."

He shrugged. "I feel sorry for the kids. I doubt it's any happier a household than it was when I was a kid." He huffed, almost self-consciously. "I don't know why, after eons, that's suddenly come back to me."

I went over to hug him and he wrapped me up tightly but carefully. "Because you care."

He dipped his nose to my ear. "I do care, Wren. I never knew it was possible to care as much as I do."

I was filled with this fluttery happiness that had little to do with heartburn and everything to do with the guy I'd spend the rest of time with.

As I looked at him, I lay my hand on his cheek. "It's okay to be scared."

He huffed self-deprecatingly. "I'm terrified."

I nodded. "Me too. But we'll work it out together."

There was a ghost of a smile on his face.

"What wrong?" Kyle asked and I turned to look at him.

"We haven't told the boys," I said to Drake.

He looked almost surprised. "We haven't."

"Told what?" Kyle asked, cocking his head to the side. Kitty sat by his side, its tale curling around Kyle almost protectively. Kyle had finally taken off his snorkel and mask.

"Do you want to tell him?" Drake asked.

"You can, but where are the others?"

"You rang?" Truman asked, swirling his mojito.

"Boss? Boss-lady?" Ignacio grunted.

"Great. Now we're all here…" Drake said stiltedly. "Wren's pregnant."

There was a slight pause, then everything happened at once.

Kyle launched himself at me, chittering in excitement.

Truman gave a, "Mazel tov," with a raise of his glass.

And Ignacio nodded in approval, a slight smirk at one corner of his lips.

"A baby?" Kyle said as he looked up at me, hanging onto my legs.

I nodded. "A baby."

"Just the one," Drake said quickly and I laughed.

"Just the one," Kyle repeated with a nod, reaching up to press his ear to my stomach.

"I don't know if you can hear anything yet," I told him gently.

"Heartbeat," he said definitively.

I blinked. "Really?"

He nodded against me. "Strong."

I looked to Drake and he shrugged. "Devilbums have unnecessarily good hearing."

"All the better to hear you with, sir," Truman said.

I smiled at him. "Brushing up on your fairy tales?"

He inclined his head. "Indeed, ma'am. But none of this Grimm brothers' nonsense. Baby will no doubt be far more interested in the originals."

I was going to argue that no baby of mine needed to know about death and mayhem and witches and wolves. But who was I kidding? It was Lucifer's grandchild, may as well get a head start on all that stuff.

"Exactly," Drake said, kissing the side of my head.

"Get out of my head," I replied.

"Sorry."

"Shit!"

"What?"

"We should tell my family."

Drake nodded. "We should. Do you want to tell them in person?"

I thought about it. It seemed to make the most sense. Plus it had been a while since I'd seen them, for me. "Probably."

"Okay. Send them a letter and invite them down."

"Just invite them down?" I laughed.

"Yeah. Dad's already made them their own door. Just give them the time and we'll have them around."

"I will make a cake," Truman offered.

Kyle was still hugging my legs so all I could do while I tried not to overbalance was nod and say, "Thank you."

"Let's invite your family down," Drake said, giving me an encouraging smile.

I nodded and set to prying Kyle's excitement off me so I could go and write them a letter.

Letters were the most reliable form of communication between Earth and Hell. We were partially breaking the embargo, but Thane had been happy to play postman so, strictly, we weren't breaking anything.

Thane seemed particularly happy to play postman when I had a letter to send to Harmony. But I wasn't going to read too much into that. What Harmony and Thane did and didn't get up to wasn't my business until if and when they decided to tell me about it.

When Thane came to pick up the letter, we, of course, told him the news as well.

"Really?" Thane chuckled roughly, picking me up into a hug belying how weak he looked.

Not that he was overly sickly looking, but he wasn't a muscly guy. Gangly was a more accurate description.

"Really," Drake told him.

"Have you told Cadriel?"

"No yet," was Drake's stony reply.

"What's wrong with telling Cadriel?" I asked.

"Oh, he'll take the absolute piss." Thane put me down again, laughing. "Dude, you are in for teasing and disapproval until the end days!"

Drake huffed. "I'm aware."

Thane chuckled to himself quite happily as Drake got stonier and stonier. I bit my lip to stop myself laughing as well and held the letter out for Thane.

"Maybe you should take this up?" I asked.

Thane nodded. "I probably should. Reap you later."

"Bye."

With the materialisation of his scythe and robes, he was gone, melting into the shadows like he never existed.

"I presume we're hiding this from Cadriel as long as possible?" I asked Drake, still trying not to laugh.

He nodded. "I'm surprised he doesn't already know."

Cadriel didn't find out for the next couple of weeks, then I was opening the side door to let my family in.

"Wren!" Mum cried, throwing her arms around me.

"Mum, hi." I laughed and nodded to Dad and Tilly. "Thanks for coming, guys."

"I've got the kettle on," Truman said. "Can I get anyone a hot drink? Something stronger, perhaps?"

I looked at Mum. "Truman's mojitos are a real pleasure."

Mum and Tilly said they'd try one, but Dad thought he'd best stick with a coffee, and I opted for tea. Truman nodded and hurried off to the kitchen.

A clatter behind me drew all eyes.

"Bad Kitty. Off furniture," Kyle told the mandagot.

Its tale swished as it took in the three newcomers.

I cleared my throat. "Kitty, these are family. And remember what we said about family?"

"No eating," Kyle said with a nod, looking at Kitty pointedly.

"At least my pet is caged," Ignacio said as he stepped out from behind the couch.

I sighed, "True. Bessie is at least contained."

"No cage Kitty," Kyle said firmly.

I smiled at him. "No one's going to cage Kitty, Kyle."

"It seems like you have your hands full here," Dad said as I led them all to sit down.

I nodded. "It's busy, that's for sure."

"Your letter said you've been working with…baby devilbums?" Tilly asked, her eyes darting to Kitty warily.

"Yes." I nodded. "It's like training sixty Kyle's all at once, but they've got less understanding."

Tilly laughed. "Ouch."

"Yeah."

"But, fun?"

I nodded again. "So fun."

"Brian," Drake said as he walked in. "Sam. Tilly. How are you?"

"Oh, fine. Thanks," Dad said, shaking his hand.

Drake kissed Mum's and Tilly's cheeks.

"Please, sit."

We all dropped to sitting.

"The house is lovely," Mum said warmly as she looked around.

"I can show you around later if you like?"

"That would be wonderful."

"So, how are things?" Dad asked as Truman brought in the drinks and some cake on a tray.

I looked to Drake. "Well, we've got some news."

Mum's eyes shone. Tilly got a knowing smirk. And Dad was busy with the cake.

"News?" Mum asked failing at nonchalance.

Drake took my hand but, before he could say anything, Kyle sang, "Going to get a baby!"

Mum squealed in excitement. Tilly cheered. And Dad looked up with a mouthful of cake and said, "Baby?"

Drake and I nodded.

"I'm pregnant," I said.

"Oh, that's wonderful!" Mum said.

"So exciting," Tilly agreed.

Dad looked between us as though he was confused. Then, he started smiling as he got up. He pulled Drake off the couch and gave him a big hug.

"Great news. Congratulations."

Drake chuckled roughly as he shot me a look.

I smiled and shrugged.

We spent the next hour or so talking about what we'd all been up to, how exciting the baby news was, which room would be the nursery, how often the humans would be able to come and see it, and soon the tour of the house was forgotten in favour of more thrilling things.

"It does of course mean I kind of have powers now…" I was saying to Tilly.

"What? No freaking way?"

I nodded. "Way. But it comes with some…less good news."

"Less good?"

Now, I had everyone's attention. Well, I supposed they may as well know the risks we might be in for.

I cleared my throat. "So…turns out carrying a Nephilim kid isn't awesome. Even a part-Nephilim baby is going to potentially have…complications."

"What kind of complications?" Dad asked, concerned.

Drake squeezed my hand and we shared a look.

I knew about the basics about how dangerous carrying a Nephilim was, but I didn't know the specifics.

So, I'd spent the last couple of weeks researching Nephilim births as well as practising to see if I had any other cool powers. While the powers were cool, the potential complications were slightly more pressing.

Turns out that nine times out of ten, the mother didn't survive and the baby survived only six of those times. That Drake and his mother had survived was a literal miracle of some kind. Though, I very much doubted it had anything to do with Drake's grandfather.

"If the baby survives, it might kill me," I said simply.

I could my family needed time to process that.

"Kill you?" Dad asked.

"If it survives?" Mum asked.

"That sucks," Tilly said. Her tone made me think she'd been hanging out with Harmony a lot lately.

I nodded, but it was Drake who answered.

"It's not ideal and being here should help her. The residual power of my father *should* keep her safe."

"Should?" Tilly looked at him like she needed answers and she needed them yesterday.

"I can't speak in absolutes. I won't. The fact is, we don't know. There has never been a half-Nephilim. Not as far as anyone knows. There are no rules on this."

"But the risk is less because it's only part-Nephilim?"

Drake nodded. "That I can guarantee, but we don't know the numbers."

Dad seemed to think about that for a moment. "Okay."

"Okay?" I clarified.

"Okay." Dad nodded. "I trust you to keep her safe. I trust your father to keep her safe. I trust the boys to keep her safe.

Heck, at a pinch, I trust your grandfather to keep her safe. I know she'll be fine and so will the baby."

I smiled at my family, wondering how I'd got so lucky to have such a supportive family. I knew they were looking forward to having a baby to coddle, but it was more than that. They legitimately believed I could do anything I put my mind to.

It bolstered my confidence more than I could say.

I was slightly less terrified now of having my body literally ripped to shreds during the birthing process. I had all of Hell on my side. Somehow, we'd get through this.

After all, I was Lucifer's daughter-in-law and I didn't lose.

Drake

"Can we go over this one more time?" I asked as I looked at the boys.

We were standing in the front hallway. Kyle sat on the mandagot's back, wearing a backpack and an explorer's hat. Ignacio held a pike and a shield with a gorgon head on it. Truman was just Truman, hands behind his back and waiting to be dismissed.

"Cross the river," Ignacio said gruffly.

"Where to?" I asked.

"To Elysium."

"Which river?"

"Okeanos."

"How do you get over it?"

"Ask Charon to take us across, sir."

I nodded to Truman. "Good. Who do we watch out for?"

"Rhadamanthus, judge of the dead," Truman said.

"Because he'll send us back," Ignacio said.

"Good. Then what?"

"Sneaking in Elysium," Kyle sang.

"Ignore the golden gates," Ignacio added.

"And to the secret door," Truman finished.

"And what do we do when we get to the secret door?"

"Beat up any angels who won't let us in," Ignacio said, brandishing his pike.

I looked up at Wren, who was standing on the stairs and ready to say goodbye to the boys.

"But no killing." Kyle shook his head.

I was seriously rethinking this plan. What had I been on to even suggest sending the boys to Heaven to tell Grandad about the baby? Because three devilbums in Heaven was totally going to go unnoticed.

"That's right. No killing," Wren said. "What do we do instead?"

"Sneaky quick to find Grandad," Kyle said. "Hide from all the angels."

I nodded. "The less beings who see you the better. Who do we particularly have to avoid?"

"Michael," Truman said.

"If we see him, we stab him," Ignacio grunted.

I shared another look with Wren and sighed.

"No. No stabbing Michael." I pointed at Ignacio to stop him arguing. "No matter how much we want to. No stabbing Michael. In and out. Quick and quiet. Yes?"

"Yes!" Kyle nodded enthusiastically.

Ignacio huffed grumpily but nodded.

Truman sighed. "Very well, sir."

"All right. I think you're ready."

"You boys be safe and be back as quick as you can, okay?" Wren looked at them all seriously.

"Home soon," Kyle promised as he and the mandagot headed for the door.

"Keep him out of trouble," I said to the others.

Ignacio nodded and followed Kyle.

I sighed and looked at Truman. "Keep them both out of trouble, sir?"

I nodded. "Please."

"I'll do my best, sir. We'll be home quick smart."

"Be sure you are," Wren said.

"I will, ma'am." He nodded goodbye to her and then the three of them were gone.

Wren came down the rest of the stairs and hugged me. "They'll be okay."

I took a deep breath. "I'm sure you're right."

"You can still worry about them."

"What a relief," I said sarcastically.

"Do you need to go and see Cadriel?"

"What would I possibly need to see Cadriel about?"

"I hear pain helps."

"Have you been spending too much time with Ignacio?" I asked.

"Define too much time," she laughed.

I hugged her tightly. "You might be right, though."

"Go and hang out with Cadriel. I'll be fine on my own."

"Promise?" I checked.

I felt her nod. "Promise."

I took another breath. "All right. I won't be too long."

"Do what you've got to do. Pummel good. Be pummelled good. Whatever you need."

I looked at her and had to wonder how I'd been so lucky. Here was a woman who didn't shy away from any part of me. No matter how dark that part might be. I was never at risk of being anything but myself with anyone, but to have her accept and want all of me was gratifying.

I kissed her hard, putting everything I was feeling into one kiss rather than bothering with words. Her arms wound around my neck and she kissed me back hungrily. But, as much as I liked any private time we spent together, I needed pain to take my mind of worrying about the boys.

Gently, I pulled away from her.

"I'll see you later."

"Okay."

Wren looked into my eyes as she cupped my cheek. It was a supportive action and one I wasn't used to after so many years without it.

I pulled myself away from her before I forgot what I was doing and went to find Cadriel. He was in the colosseum usually reserved for Tussle Tuesdays. He was training two other Grigori.

"Using our resources for your own means?" I called down, leaning on the wall.

Cadriel looked over, spread his arms out wide and smirked ruefully. "Who am I to disobey the embargo?"

I scoffed. "How many times have you snuck in and out of Earth since the embargo started?"

Cadriel shrugged as he winged his was over to me. "I can't say I've been keeping track."

I nodded. "Enough, then."

"You here looking for a fight?"

"If you're not too busy with those guys?"

"What about you? Aren't you busy with preparations for a mewling waste of space?"

I frowned at him, but it was only half-hearted. "I was one of those mewling wastes of space once."

"And I thank all mercies I didn't meet you then." He looked me over. "You look stressed. Is it just this baby thing or is something else bothering you?"

"The boys are sneaking into Heaven to pass the news onto my grandfather–"

"Without me?" he asked incredulously.

"You are far less easy to hide. Besides, you wouldn't get past the golden gates."

He nodded. "Fair. One look at Michael's smug face and I'd feel duty bound to carve it off for him."

"And that's nothing on if you ran into Samael."

He stepped towards the two fighting Grigori. "All right. Step aside. Let two masters show you how it's done!"

I gave a crooked smile. "Calling me a master, now? What next? Did you pick up some stray manners?"

He shrugged as he rose into the air. "Manners, me? Never."

I rose with him. "Perhaps you've learnt to appreciate your friends, then?"

Cadriel barked a laugh. "If I have to be nice to my friends, I've got the wrong friends."

I smiled and nodded, agreeing with him there. Part of what worked so well for us was the ability to mercilessly tease each other and beat each other to a bloody pulp when we felt like it. It might have been a bit weird for some friendships, but it worked for ours.

The other two Grigori passed us their weapons and got out of the way for us.

"Any requests?" Cadriel asked as we circled.

His wings flapped restlessly behind him so I didn't bother putting mine away.

"Just distract me, Grigori."

"With pleasure, Morningstar."

Despite wielding a mace that was anything but his preferred weapon, Cadriel didn't let it slow him down one bit. He swung at me almost before I had a chance to prepare.

"You're getting slower, Morningstar," he said as we fought. "Perhaps you need to spend less time in bed with your *wife* and more time in training."

I smirked. "Just because you want a human of your own."

"Oh, I want far more than one human of my own. I have a planet full of them to choose from."

"And if you met the right human?"

"Humans are too breakable for the long-term. You should be intimately aware of this. Now especially."

I paused and the mace crashed into my stomach, sending me sprawling into the dust. I looked up at him, standing there and gloating as he looked down at me.

"What?" was all I was capable of saying.

"There is a pool going to see how long it takes for that baby to kill her."

I jumped up, beyond worried and onto pissed off. "What did you say?"

"The pool? My bet was childbirth."

I ran at him, but he was ready for me. He grabbed my front and swept us both into the air. My wings burst again and sent us spinning.

"You bet on my wife to die?" I snapped.

He shrugged, totally unapologetic. "She's human, Drake. What do you expect?"

"What did Thane say?"

"About what?"

"About if this was going to kill her."

"He doesn't know."

"He doesn't know or he won't say?"

Cadriel shrugged again. "I don't know. But he said he didn't know."

I frowned. "How can he not know?"

But Cadriel wasn't interested in discussing the philosophy behind what or why Thane did or didn't know something. While I was distracted, he grabbed a firmer hold of me and threw me to the ground.

I crashed into the dust, feeling at least one bone crack along with the ground under me. The air raced from my lungs.

Cadriel landed over me, seized the front of my shirt in his hand and pulled me up towards him. "Are you here to fight or are you just here to debate? I'm sure I could find Xenophanes for you. Or maybe Heraclitus is more to your mood?"

I shoved him off me, using my wings for leverage. "You are perilously close to crossing a line, Grigori," I hissed.

He chuckled humourlessly. "It is in my nature to cross lines, Morningstar," he reminded me. "I need not follow rules set by your precious humans or your grandfather."

There was no use arguing with him. He was right. Grigori lived by their own set of rules. Well, they were more like guidelines. They basically did what they wanted and, as long as the didn't break any of the cosmic no-nos that governed all entities in creation, then no one could really stop them. Azazel would try, but that wasn't going to change anything.

I twirled the sword in my hand and Cadriel did the same with his mace as we started circling again.

"There it is," he purred. "That fire. Nothing to do with humanity, that."

I knew he was goading me. He was pretty much always goading me. And I pretty much always rose to the bait. This time was no exception.

With a growl that was more a roar, I flung myself at him and we traded blows. Many hit their target, many were blocked. We eventually did away with weapons and were just happy to use our bare hands.

The gaping wounds on my body were rubbed with dirt. The ground beneath us was slippery with blood. And still we fought. We fought until I could feel nothing but the thready beat of my blood fighting to course through my emptying veins. We fought until Cadriel swayed on his feet.

At the same time, we both dropped to our knees, swayed for a moment, then collapsed.

I breathed heavily and heard him doing the same.

"For what it's worth," he huffed, "I lied."

"About what this time?" I panted.

"My bet."

I gave a breathy laugh. "You gave her six months?"

"No. I bet she'd live."

I twisted my head on the ground to look at him. "You did?"

He nodded. "Your wife's strong. Stronger than I think any of us gives her credit for. She won't let a little thing like a murderous parasite be the end of her."

"Charming way of describing my child."

"True," he chuckled. "It's yours, so it'll be more like a snake."

I flailed my arm uselessly in his direction as I looked back up at the ceiling. "Shut up."

"If you're happy, I'm happy for you, Drake."

I nodded. "Thanks, man."

"How scared are you?"

"Terrified."

"She'll make it."

"I'm less worried she won't and more worried about my ability to parent. I don't exactly have the best example to follow when it comes to being a dad."

Another humourless chuckle. "Mine's not great either, so don't come to me looking for advice."

"I wasn't planning on it."

"Good. But I still get to be the fun uncle who brings it swords for its birthday."

"I think you'll have to get in line behind Ignacio."

"The boys excited?"

"Kyle is. He's already moved most of his toys into the room we've designated as the nursery."

"What's he going to play with then?"

"Oh, they're still his. They're going to share."

Cadriel's laugh was slightly humoured this time. "Of course, they are. It'll be like having two kids."

I shrugged, a tired smile on my face. "Why not."

"At least it might keep Kyle out of some trouble."

"More like double the trouble."

"You're going to need around the clock babysitting."

"I know."

"For both of them."

My smile grew. "I know."

We lay in silence for a bit longer, until the worst of our injuries had stopped gushing and our blood supplies were restored enough we weren't going to pass out just by standing up.

Wren

I didn't know him, but I felt like I knew him more intimately than I'd ever known another being.

He was gorgeous. More than gorgeous. My mind went blank just looking at him. Flowing dark blond hair framed a chiselled face. His eyes were like a sparkling, clam sea on a summer's day. He wore nothing but linen trousers, his muscular body on full display in the bright, warm sun.

"Who are you?" I asked him, looking around.

We were standing in a… It was either a garden or a forest of some kind. There were flowers and creepers and it was all overgrown, but not in an untended way. It was like it was just too lush and beautiful to tame. There was a faint breeze that brought hints of lavender and frangipani to my nose.

"Where am I?"

He took a step towards me and I felt myself do the same as though I was drawn to him.

"The garden," he answered cryptically.

"I can see that," I said with a smile. "What garden? How did I get here?"

"All in due time. You are safe now, Serenity."

I sure did feel safe. I felt the safest I'd ever felt in my life. But there was this sense I couldn't shake that something wasn't right. I was supposed to be somewhere else. I was supposed to be with someone else. But I couldn't remember where. I couldn't remember who.

The guy held his hand out to me and I reached forward to take it. I noticed I was wearing a flowing white dress. Something about that seemed odd, but I couldn't place why.

His hand was warm in mine and I looked up into his eyes. I felt a fluttering tingle zip through my body as he drew me closer to him.

"I can protect you, Serenity. Better than him."

I frowned, but there was smile a serene smile on my face. "Better than who? Who are you?"

He leant towards me and ran his nose over my cheek. I closed my eyes as he kissed my neck. I leant into him as his other hand skimmed down my side and pulled my hips against him. I felt him hard, pressing into me and filling me with a deep need for him.

His hand ran back up my body to cup my breast as he finally whispered in my ear, "Aksel."

As I opened my eyes, something felt different. I was in bed. I was in my room. My husband was by my side.

My dream left fragments of feeling floating around my mind and my body. It was weird. I felt this pull to whoever Aksel was. My body needed him. I needed him to finished what he started. But I also didn't want him anywhere near my body, thank you very much.

I breathed out heavily as I tried to calm the racing of my heart and shove Aksel out of my mind.

"Who the fuck is Aksel?" came Drake's gravelly morning voice.

I turned to look at him. "I don't know," I said honestly.

Drake's eyes were bright red as the bored into mine even though they still looked half-glassy with sleep.

He drew my chin towards him. "Do you remember what I told you would happen if you dreamt about someone else?" he asked me, his voice low and meaningful.

My body was already at attention, it was ready to jump at the sound of his voice. I bite my lip and nodded slowly.

"You told me you'd wipe all memory of him from my mind," I said.

He nodded. "I did."

He slid his hand down my body, stopping to rest on my stomach.

The glow in his eyes softened for a moment as he looked at me.

"But I'm going to have to be more careful with you than I'd planned."

I smiled. "Really?"

He nodded again. "Yes."

"What did you have in mind then?"

Drake lay back and crooked a finger at me. "I feel like it would be safe with you on top."

"Oh, safer?" I teased as I slid onto him, my legs straddling his hips.

"Safer."

His hand ran up my leg slowly until his thumb gently traced over my clit. I breathed in deeply and was glad the boys were still on their mission so we had all the time we wanted.

Drake started rubbing me slowly, just the way he knew I liked. There was no teasing, there was no working his way up. Drake wanted me thinking of nothing but him and he was going the most direct way about it.

My hips started rocking in time with his rhythm and I braced against his chest as I breathed deeply. I didn't want that delicious build up to stop, but I also wanted more.

"Who are you thinking of now, Wren?" he asked me.

"You," I told him.

"Anyone else?"

I shook my head as I ground against his hand. The pleasure built in me and I could feel myself teetering on the precipice, just waiting to tumble over.

"And who do you cum for?"

"Only you."

My legs tensed around him as I came hard. Drake lazily ran his fingers over me as the last waves hit. Then he sat up quickly and wrapped his arms around me. I put my arms around his neck and leant my forehead to his as I got my breath back.

"You know I can't help who I dream about," I reminded him.

His eyes were still bright red as they stared deep into mine. "I do know that. I'm still going to take your mind of anyone else who makes their way in there, though."

I smiled and kissed him, then pulled away to look at him as I lifted myself up and slid back down onto his erection.

He let out a long, slow breath as I did. He was both helping me support my weight and holding me so I didn't go too quickly.

We just stayed like that for a few moments, kissing each other softly and feeling in no hurry to rush things.

Slowly, I started moving against him and I felt him thrust his hips to meet me. It was languid and gentle, filling me with a deep satisfaction that wasn't just physical. And I didn't have to be able to read his mind to know he felt it too.

So, we kept an unhurried pace, holding each other tight and our kisses full of passion and love. Now and then, he'd murmur my name or I his, or his lips would trail to my neck only to find their way back to my lips again.

As we both got closer, our pace increased and we held each other tighter. Kisses were forgotten in lieu of giving ourselves over completely to the feelings building.

He came first with a primal groan, and that was enough to send me over the edge with a moan of my own.

Drake showered me in kisses as we moved together lazily and more slowly, and finally just held each other.

I felt him smiling against my lips.

"What?" I asked.

He shook his head. "I was just imagining things."

"What things?"

He huffed a rough laugh as he brushed my hair back. "For a minute, I thought I saw your eyes glow."

We both froze and stopped to look at each other.

"You don't think...?" I asked.

He shook his head, but didn't look convinced. "That's a celestial thing, but not something it would pass on. I don't think?"

I shrugged as I started to get off him. He made a noise of complaint, but only helped me keep my balance so I didn't fall off the bed – it wouldn't have been the first time.

"How many souls do you need to torture today?" I asked as I pulled my hair up before heading to the bathroom.

"Depends on how badly behaved everyone's been."

"So..." I started. "Does that mean, five? A hundred?"

"Maybe twenty personal hells?" Drake mused from the bedroom.

"How many are there?"

"Infinite."

"Who mans them when you're busy with other souls?"

"Demons. With the more and more souls we get every Earth day, we need more demons. Luckily, not only is Hell excellent at torment, but we're also very good at spitting out more demons to handle those souls."

"So, it really is like a huge factory," I said as I walked back into the bedroom to find he'd got dressed.

He nodded. "Something like that, yeah. Only way more efficient." He stepped over and kissed me quickly. "What are your plans for the day?"

I shrugged as I started getting dressed. "I said something about going to see your dad. Seph and I were going to get some lunch. Harmony was going to pop down for a bit at some point. And, I need to check in on Pike."

"Pike?"

I nodded. "Mm. My baby devilbum."

Drake stepped up behind me and wrapped me up in his arms. "Your baby devilbum," he teased and I heard the smile in his voice. "Just how many kids are we going to end up with?"

I turned to face him and slid my arms around his neck. "I couldn't tell you. We do have the rest of time, after all."

He tried to fight a wider smile and failed. "And I just can't say no to you."

I reached up to kiss him. "You shouldn't have told me that. I'm going to use that to my every advantage."

"Oh, are you?" he said with no attempt to hide his smile.

I nodded. "I am."

"Well, I guess I'd best just get used to it then."

He let me go and we trailed downstairs.

"Walk you to the throne room?" he asked.

I nodded. "Sounds good."

He took my hand and we strolled to his father's throne room.

When we got there, Lucifer was rehearsing a new performance. The unicycle-riding, juggling rolly-polly demon was back, as was what looked like a demonic monkey and some ghostly-looking horses. One horse was balancing on a ball. Another had a ball on its nose. And the monkey was playing the bagpipes. Lucifer was in the middle of them all, directing them in a navy blue and white pinstripe suit with a straw boater hat perched off-kilter on his head.

"What are you doing now?" Drake asked, exasperation evident in his tone.

"Trying out a new welcome show," Lucifer explained without turning around.

"Why are you doing that?"

"Because I feel like fire and brimstone might be getting a little bit old. What do you think?"

"I think you're having a mid-life crisis," Drake answered. "Obviously the apocalypse is closer than we thought."

Lucifer turned quickly. "Don't even joke about things like that, son!" he hissed, looking around quickly as though just saying the word was going to make it appear.

"Oh, for Grandad's…" Drake muttered. "You don't even know who the anti-Christ is, do you?"

Lucifer shook out his shoulders. "Well, no."

Drake nodded. "No. So, let's not get quite so freaked out by saying the word apocalypse down here."

"Why do you care anyway?" I asked. "I thought you wanted Hell on Earth?"

"The anti-Christ is supposed to be more powerful than him or Grandad. Neither of them want him being born and making them inferior," Drake explained.

"You make us sound so fickle, son."

Even I looked at Lucifer like he needed to rethink that sentence.

"Yes. All right," he admitted. "I see your point. Now, Drake. Don't you have places to be, souls to torture?"

"Yes." He kissed my head and squeezed my hand. "I'll see you later."

I nodded. "Okay."

"Look after her," he said to his father.

Lucifer crossed his chest. "On my life."

Drake left and Lucifer conjured me a chair to sit and watch his rehearsals for a while. Finally, after what had to be the hundredth, 'No, Whiskey. How many times do I have to tell you this is a PG-13 show? Did Tallulah even consent?' they were all dismissed and Lucifer dropped next to me. Luckily a chair appeared to catch him before he hit the floor.

"You look hungry, Wren," Lucifer sighed. "What can I get you?"

"Apple something," I replied without thinking.

"Apple something?"

I nodded. "I don't care what it is, but I just need apples."

Neville nodded – and I hadn't even realised Neville was in the room. "Hell'll do that to you."

I looked at him in confusion.

"Apples," Lucifer said, like that was an answer. "Apples are kind of our thing?"

I frowned. "In what way?"

"Garden of Eden. Adam and Eve. Big ol' snake. Any of this ringing any bells?" Lucifer asked.

That it did. "Oh. Right. Yes. Okay. Got it. So pregnancy cravings. Apples, huh?"

Lucifer nodded. "Yes. I hear it's particularly common of those who have lain with Fallen."

"Does that make Drake–?"

"Oh. Not really. He and I are on a timeout, so to speak. But we're not technically fallen." He released his pure white wings and ruffled them proudly. "Hence the wings."

"I see." I sort of did see, but that did not negate the fact I was starving and all I wanted was… "Apple crumble."

"Apple crumble?" Lucifer said appreciatively. "One apple crumble for my daughter-in-law and my grandchild. Coming up."

I smiled at him and decided there were definitely perks to carrying the Devil's grandchild.

9

Drake

I had an unusual spring in my step as I went about my day.

It might have been Wren's growing belly. It might have been the fact that my father hadn't sung at me in weeks. It might even have been that the torture had been particularly bloody and gory as of late. But I suspected it was mainly because the boys had finally organised my 'sindig'.

We were all getting together – this time without any truth – there was going to be blood and battles and loud music. There would be demons and ghosts of all varieties, all celebrating in the way only Hellspawn could.

But first, I had to get through the rest of my day.

Anything and everything seemed to be going wrong.

There was a clown standing in the middle of the Asphodel Fields, all its fluoro colours sticking out like a sore thumb against the drab grey background of the ancient field. And it didn't want to move. It was convinced it belonged there.

Every time I tried herding it out, it would slowly turn around and return to its position, silent as anything, just holding the string of its bright pink and green balloon.

"All right, Drake?" I heard the familiar voice behind me as I stared at the clown.

"Yeah, not really, Larry." I pointed at the clown as Larry hovered beside me. "I can't get it to go back to its field."

Larry floated towards it and looked it over. The clown blinked unnaturally slowly, then turned and started ambling away purposelessly.

I didn't have to walk very fast to keep up with it.

"What's it doing?" I asked Larry.

"I'd say it fell in the Lethe," he answered.

I looked at him. "Demons don't fall in the Lethe."

Larry waved his incorporeal hand over its face. It just kept walking and walked right though Larry's outstretched arm. Larry looked around at all the shades in the field. They were all the same. Those same blank expressions, vacant eyes. No one was home and only the safety light was on.

The Asphodel Field had always given me the heebie-jeebies. Blood and screaming, I was your guy. But this was just…so much, endless nothing. I could almost feel it clawing at me, threatening to take me to join it.

I looked towards the Lethe.

It had that effect on humans. It called to you. It wanted you to bathe in it. To forget everything you were on Earth. It was like everything you were in life fed it in some undamned way.

It made my skin crawl.

"Okay," I said quickly, pulling myself together. "Say it did fall in the Lethe. How and why?"

"Gosh, I couldn't answer that one, Drake. Maybe it wanted a bath and got confused."

I frowned at Larry. "Since when do demons worry about baths?"

"Kyle's quite fond of baths."

"Kyle's not exactly the perfect example of your average demon."

The clown was still wandering aimlessly. At this point, I was surprised it still had hold of its balloon to be honest.

There was something going on with the Lethe. Something not quite right. It hadn't wiped Wren's memory, but it had wiped a demon's. A demon who was now bound to wander the Asphodel Fields aimlessly for the rest of time.

And there was nothing I could do. Even my father couldn't return you after you'd given your life to the Lethe. Well, I wasn't a hundred percent certain on that. More likely he wouldn't. But amounted to the same thing.

All I could do was make a note of it and move on for the day.

When everything was finally sorted out and I was home and changed, Cadriel appeared in our front room ready to take me to my 'sindig'.

"You boys have a good night, but not too good. Okay?" Wren said with a wry smile.

"I make no promises for the Nephilim," Cadriel said.

Wren nodded as though she expected as much. "All right. Go on, then."

"What are you doing tonight?"

"I'm going to snuggle up with a cup of tea and read a book," she replied. "Now get going so I can have some time to myself."

We said our goodbyes and I ushered us out.

"Your wife is bossy," Cadriel noted as we walked.

"She is."

"She belongs."

"She does."

"You ready, Morningstar?"

"As I'll ever be, Grigori."

Cadriel clapped me on the back as we walked into the great cavern. It was decorated in the most Hellish of ways.

Souls provided the lighting – with either a candle on their decapitated head, or holding one in each hand with another in their mouth. Others were piled up and set alight for bonfires.

Some souls even provided some music. Four of them played their entrails in an otherworldly string quartet. The music was appropriately haunting.

Demons danced and swayed to the music, stomping around the bonfires in primal ways. Others fucked – either each other or the tormented souls – unabashed wherever they were, limbs entwined with others in numerous orgies around the cavern as beings danced around them.

"What do you think?" Cadriel asked, looking at me for my reaction.

"Exactly what I'd expect from the perfect 'sindig'," I replied.

And it was. This was how Hell did celebrations. You got that big promotion? 'Sindig'. You tortured your five thousandth soul? 'Sindig'. There hadn't been a good 'sindig' in a while? 'Sindig'.

We got caught up in the festivities for a while, passing around food and wine. We met up with Thane and Samyeza and danced until we fell in a pile in the corner so we could keep watching the others while we talked.

"How is it up there?" I asked, knowing full-well that 'up' was a loose construct.

Thane shook his head noncommittally. "It's teetering."

"Teetering how?"

"The humans are on the verge of imploding after your dad's behaviour or going back to normal," Samyeza answered for him.

"So, the embargo is still in full swing, then?"

"Michael is personally in a fucking flap about it," Cadriel said with a gleeful smirk. "He's popping down every now and then and stressing out about what they can do about it."

"About what?"

"About the clean-up."

"Clean-up?"

Samyeza inclined his head. "Michael thinks he is on 'damage control' after your father's actions."

"And has he talked to Grandad about it?"

Thane scoffed. "One of those winged idiots actually talk to God about something? No. Of course not. What if their standing orders for the past few eons suddenly change? They couldn't possibly have that!"

"I thought you were a neutral body?" Cadriel asked him suspiciously.

Thane nodded. "I am."

"That doesn't sound very neutral."

"Oh, no. I think all of you are equally incompetent and useless," Thane joked.

Cadriel threw a passing devilbum at him.

"Excuse me," the devilbum chuckled nervously then ran off like he thought Thane was going to reap him then and there.

Thane grinned, looking a little more ghastly than usual.

"How's Wren?" he asked.

I huffed. "Other than a reoccurring dream about someone called Aksel, she's good."

Samyeza sat up. "Aksel?"

I looked at him. "You know an Aksel?"

"I know *the* Aksel."

"I don't like the sound of that."

"Nor should you."

"Wait," Cadriel said. "You don't mean the cupid Aksel?"

Samyeza inclined his head again. "I do."

Thane spluttered in his drink. "*The* cupid Aksel?"

"Who is the cupid Aksel?" I asked.

"He is the second in command to Cupid himself," Samyeza said.

"What's Wren doing dreaming about Cupid's second-in-command?" Thane asked.

"I do not know. But I doubt it is a coincidence."

"You think he's doing it?" Cadriel asked.

"He has the power. But whether he would or not is another matter."

"If he was, it would be on orders," I said. "He'd have no reason or inclination to mess with my wife otherwise."

"Why would the cupids be interested in Wren?" Thane mused.

"I see no reason for them to be," Samyeza said. "I cannot see why they would be interested in the human wife of the Morningstar's son. God himself was at the wedding, that should have been enough for them to leave you both be for many centuries at least."

"What if she's not totally human anymore?" Cadriel asked.

"What do you know?"

Cadriel shrugged. "Nothing. But I know the kid's leaking powers. Maybe they think it's her?"

"Maybe she was fated for someone else and they're coming to put her on the right path?" Thane wondered.

Three sets of wings burst open and we all stood over him menacingly.

He held his hands up. "It was *just* a suggestion, guys. I'm spit-balling here. Crossing off ridiculous theories and the like."

Cadriel, Samyeza and I stood over him for a moment longer, then our wings folded and we sat back down.

"Have you any idea why the cupids would be coming for her?" Samyeza asked Thane.

He shook his head. "I can see no reason why anyone 'up' there would care about either of you. I mean, it's the first half-Nephilim kid that anyone knows of. But there's no reason to think it'll be stronger than your average Nephilim."

We all shared a look. I wasn't sure what question we were asking, but it felt like we were all wondering the same thing.

And, just like I didn't know what it was we were wondering, we all seemed to decide whatever it was was ridiculous.

We all chuckled roughly.

"No," Cadriel said.

"No way," Thane agreed.

"Impossible," Samyeza said.

"Exactly." I nodded.

We looked around at each other again. I still didn't know exactly what we'd decided was impossible, but we certainly didn't let it get in the way of us having a good rest of the night.

10

Wren

I had to hand it to Lucifer, he was taking this whole grandparent-to-be thing incredibly seriously.

But then I saw his next project and I wondered how seriously he was actually taking it.

I was about four and a half months in at this point. Apple somethings had become pretty much all I ate – and, to be fair, Lucifer had accommodated during dinner by only serving dishes with apples in them.

So, I was wandering down a tunnel, eating an apple Danish, when I saw Lucifer scurrying around. He had a bag in his hand and was taking things out of the bag to put over the points of anything pointy he found. This included weapons, rocks, teeth, demon's horns and ears, furniture, and all manner of torture devices.

I only guessed what he had in the bag when I saw Kyle coming along behind him – Kitty in tow as always – and shoving them in his mouth. Kyle seemed quite happy to climb that demon, ask another to pass it to him, or get Kitty to help him reach. But then, I knew well that Kyle would do almost anything for a marshmallow.

Lucifer stopped and looked in his bag. I could only imagine he'd run out by the look on his face. He turned around to presumably look at his handiwork only to found it all undone and Kyle standing there with his hands out a la Oliver Twist and 'please, sir'.

"Kyle! Those were for the baby!" I heard him say.

"Get baby more later. Kyle have more now?"

Lucifer stamped his foot and sighed audibly. "No. Kyle can't have more now. I'll have to find something else to baby-proof the place."

Kyle nodded his head. "'Mellows' no good. They eaten."

Lucifer looked down at Kyle. There was a hint of fondness in his annoyance. "They did get eaten. I don't suppose–" He looked up and saw me. "Ah, Serenity! How are you?"

I nodded as I brushed the apple Danish crumbs off my hands and shirt. "Fine. How are you?"

"Exasperated." He motioned for me to follow him. "Let me show you something."

Kyle waited for me to catch up to him, then took my hand in his sticky, marshmallow-covered claw. Kitty walked a little behind us.

"When did you get back?" I asked him.

"In time for 'mellows'," he said happily as he trotted along.

"Now, I have a question to ask you, Serenity," Lucifer said as we walked into the throne room. "And think about it before you just say no."

I was pretty sure it would be the sort of question I hands down said no to, but I was going to be a dutiful daughter-in-law and wait to see what he had to say.

I smiled and nodded to Persephone, who gave me a 'what's he up to now?' look. I just shrugged.

"So, I've been thinking about the cradle." Lucifer motioned for me to stop and jogged up the dais stairs to rummage behind his throne. "Persephone?" he called. "Persephone! Where did I put it?"

"Where did you put what, Hades?" she asked with a sigh, coming to stand next to me. "Hi Kyle."

"Hello." He beamed up at her.

"You look very pleased with yourself."

"'Mellows'," he said with a nod and rubbed his tummy with his free claw.

"You don't say," she mused, sharing a smile with me.

"Persephone!" Lucifer screeched again. "Where is it?"

"You'll have to be more specific," she called back.

"The cradle. It was right here."

"I don't know. Does your other wife know where you put it?" she asked drolly.

Lucifer's head appeared over his throne and he gave her a glowering sarcastic glare. "Har har. No. I'm sure I told you."

"I don't know what to tell you. I don't know what you're talking about." She shrugged as she folded her arms in front of her.

"A ha! Here it is!"

He reappeared fully, dragging a cradle with him. At least, I assumed it was a cradle because he'd said it was.

It was made out of bone and…flesh? But it was in the shape of a cradle, so I supposed that counted for something. The mobile was made of miniature severed limbs that played a haunting melody when the wind moved them.

"What do you think?" Lucifer asked proudly.

"Uh…" was about all I could muster that wasn't an immediate no.

"You love it, don't you?"

"Of course, she doesn't love it," Persephone said and you could hear the eyeroll in her tone.

"Is this true?" he asked me.

I shrugged apologetically. "It's… I don't really love it. No, sorry."

"What? Why not?" Lucifer asked, looking between us.

Kyle climbed into it with the help of Kitty. "Kyle quite like."

I spared him a smile before I was back to apologetic for Lucifer. "I just… It's not really what I had in mind I guess…?"

"Persephone!" God's voice boomed recognisably around the throne room and I could see what Lucifer thought about that.

We all turned to look at him standing in the middle of the room. He wore an impeccable light grey suit, black shoes and a black tie. His silver hair was swept back from his face, lush even despite the colour.

Persephone gave him one of her patented smirks. "Long time no see…Father."

I looked between them. "Hang on," I said. "Just hang on. How is he *your* father?"

They shared a look. God looked back to me with a shrug.

"Much like Lucifer and Hades are one…" he started, then looked to Lucifer.

"So are God and Zeus," he finished for him petulantly.

I tried getting my head around that, but my Greek mythology was a little spotty. "So, he's both your dad and your…"

"Brother." Lucifer nodded, but I could see he hated everything about it.

I was remembering what Drake said about different stories about how Lucifer ended up in Hell. In each one, God had sent him for disobedience. It seemed Lucifer wasn't just a disobedient son.

I looked at Persephone. "Which makes Persephone your wife *and* your niece?"

Persephone gave me an unapologetic look as though 'it happens'. "It gets confusing if you overthink it."

I nodded, deciding she was right and determined not to. "Okay, then."

"Gods aren't related the same way mortals are, Serenity," God told me. "Our laws, beliefs, customs are different to humanity's no matter what mythos you believe in."

I could live with that. After all, I was carrying a part-Nephilim baby. Normal laws and beliefs and customs had flown out the window months – years by now – ago.

"Excellent!" Lucifer said, pouting as he leant on the cradle of horrors. "Now that's sorted. Why are you here?"

God spread his arms out. "I was bringing these three home, of course." He pointed to Kyle and I guessed that must mean the others were around as well. "Besides, it's not every day a celestial becomes a great-grandfather."

Great-grandfather/Great-uncle?

No. Not overthinking!

"So, you show up unannounced in my domain? How would Poseidon feel if you just popped in on him? Again."

"I am ruler over all creation, son. It is my wont to see how everything is going."

"Well, it's my wont for you to bugger off. Cronos isn't that far below me. I might wake him up and see how he feels about all this."

"Cronos' sleep is so deep it would take more than you to wake him," God scoffed.

Lucifer huffed and crossed his arms. "Well, maybe. Doesn't give you the right to come barrelling in here uninvited."

"I have three devilbums and a mandagot that say otherwise."

Lucifer looked at Kyle like it was all his fault. Kyle stood up in the cradle and pointed at God.

"Told about baby," Kyle said. "We hid sneaky, sneaky. Mean angel found us. Grandad saved us."

I felt like there was far more behind his words than he was saying. But whether he was just incapable of articulating them or he hadn't fully comprehended them, I wasn't sure.

"Apologies, sir!" Truman huffed as he ran in, followed by Truman. "Uh, the Almighty Lord of the Sky has arrived, sir."

Lucifer glared at him, and spared another for Neville who ran into the back of the both of them. "I see that. What do I pay you for if not to keep unwanted visitors from the throne room?" he whinged, then pointed at God. "If I hear one more mention of you ruling over creation, I'm going to create something you're really not going to like."

God smiled. "I wouldn't dream of it."

"How long are you intending to stay?"

"Not long. I merely wanted to see the boys home safe after their…ordeal and congratulate the happy expecting couple." God turned his smile on me and I giggled like an idiot.

"Oh, thank you," I said. "Drake's working, but–"

"Might we go and find him? Persuade him to take a break maybe?"

"Excuse you!" Lucifer huffed. "Do you see me flapping on up to Heaven and telling Gabriel to take some time out of his *busy* schedule?"

"The afterlife won't grind to a halt just because we take a little time off," was God's response. "Kyle, come on. Hop out of that…thing."

"That's not a thing!" Lucifer said, his voice rising. "That is a cradle for the baby."

God looked him over carefully. "No."

"What do you mean no?"

"I mean no. You will not be putting any descendant of mine in that hideous excuse for a cot."

"Ha! Well, joke's on you, because plenty of them have been." Lucifer pointed at God like he knew without doubt that he'd just won the world's most important debate.

"Your half-demon offspring are no descendants of mine." He paused before he turned on his heel like he expected everyone to follow. "Come on, then."

Kyle jumped out of the cradle and hurried after God with Kitty in tow. Lucifer slouched after, muttering under his breath. I looked at Persephone and we fell into step together.

"This is going to be interesting isn't it?" I asked her.

Seph smirked knowingly. "It's always interesting when my father and my husband are in the same realm."

Drake

Grandad had been and, thankfully, gone. It was a tense few hours, not helped by Dad's attempt to lighten the mood with a show during dinner.

He'd pulled out all the stops. It was the full Hell experience. Marionette dancers. Tormented souls. Music that made the hair on the back of your neck stand on end and your skin crawl for no discernible reason. Grandad had been neither intimidated nor impressed.

But it was over now and we were getting on with our lives. Such as they were.

The days melted into monotony once more.

Wake up with Wren, do my rounds, do some torturing, train with Cadriel or anyone else happy to give and receive a beating, some more rounds, hope that succubus hadn't actually fallen in the Lethe, discover she had, have no idea how or why, go home to Wren, have dinner in the throne room, home again, some private time with my wife, go to sleep, and rinse and repeat.

But I didn't despise the monotony anymore. Having Wren to come home to made it better, she gave me a more positive outlook on my never-ending life. I enjoyed the torture, I enjoyed the times it let me be creative. I even didn't hate my rounds. I looked out on Hell and saw the beauty in it, I appreciated the raw mechanism that kept the place running, even if it was overseen by my father.

My father, who annoyed me to no end on a daily basis.

"Can it not wait?" I asked. "I've got another demon wandering the Asphodel Fields and someone's convinced there's noises coming from…further down."

"Tartarus?" Dad asked, looking down.

I shrugged. "There is a rumour that a Danaide is filling her jug up from the Styx."

"What? That's ridiculous!"

"That's what I said, but I also said I'd check it out."

Dad nodded. "All right, just stay away from the Lethe."

I frowned. "Why?"

"Because the last thing I need is you deciding you need a bath."

"I'm not going to decide I need a bath," I told him.

"Uh huh. You say that now. Next thing I know, you're wandering around and forgotten who you are."

"Why does it even matter to you?"

Dad snapped. And I don't mean he spoke in an angry and flippant manner. I don't mean he went cuckoo, dressed up as nun and started singing nursery rhymes. I mean he snapped.

Growing to five times his normal size, he was fire and brimstone and death. Lava ran over his skin in rivulets like veins. Great big horns protruded from his head. His wings took up most of the room. And he bared down on me, heat and the stench of death wafting over me.

"I didn't cock up Earth just for you to go and fall in the holy Lethe!" he snarled.

I blinked, in no way bothered by his transformation. His words were a different matter entirely.

"What do you mean you cocked up Earth?" I asked.

As he spoke next, he shrank back to the pinstripe-suited elegant middle-aged man he was so fond of.

"Why do you think Azazel took so long to find you? Why the Fallen gave up so quickly? Why do you think I was off pulling all those stunts despite the cosmic no-nos?"

"Because you don't give a shit about cosmic no-nos?"

Dad swept the rogue hairs back into place with a sigh. "I might not give a shit about cosmic no-nos, but is it really like me to lock myself off Earth?"

I thought about that and realised that it wasn't very like him at all. "No," I said slowly.

He shook his head. "No. So why do you think I was doing all that?"

"I couldn't begin to guess. Were you bored?"

He started flaming out, then took a deep breath and got control over himself. "I was keeping you and Wren safe," he snapped.

"What?" I scoffed. "Safe?"

"Yes. Safe," he yelled. "My entire existence now is keeping my family safe! Hence my behaviour on Earth. And now there's the embargo, and the clean-up, and Michael's constantly on me about 'proper Earth etiquette, blah blah blah'. *Now* I'm bored."

"Since when is your existence keeping your family safe?"

"Since you were born," he said, in much the same way as he was half-wishing I hadn't been and saved him all the bother.

"Oh, so killing Mum was all to keep me safe was it?" I sneered.

"I didn't kill your mother!" he shouted.

I paused for a split-second. We couldn't lie. But we could stretch the truth even better than those fae bastards. He might not have directly killed Mum, but he was responsible.

"Okay. You didn't actually deal the blow. My bad. I—"

"I had nothing to do with it other than loving her," Dad said, more quietly this time and I stopped to listen.

"What?"

"I didn't kill Maya. I wasn't even responsible for her death aside from our creating you."

"I thought Cadriel—"

"A lie Cadriel kept up for years at my behest."

"Why?"

"Because it was easier for you to hate me than have you run off and get yourself killed, son."

"If Cadriel didn't, who–?"

"Cadriel was supposed to protect you and Maya. Thane came to warn me as soon as he realised. But they hid their intention from him somehow. By the time Cadriel got there, your mother was dead and all he could do was save you and bring you here."

"Who?" I ground out, feeling my throat heat and close up.

"You know who, Drake," he said gently.

"Azazel."

Dad nodded. "I'm sorry. But I didn't want you going after him. I couldn't lose you, too."

I couldn't talk to him about this anymore. I needed space to think. I needed a minute to mourn my mother all over again. Somehow, finding out her death wasn't what I thought made it feel like losing her all over again.

"Drake?" Dad took a step towards me.

But I shook my head and stormed out.

Demons and ghosts jumped out of my way as I careened, unthinking and unseeing, through the tunnels. I wanted to hit things. I wanted to bleed. I wanted to inflict pain. But most of all, I just wanted my wife to hold me and be there with me while I processed.

I walked in the front door and slammed it shut behind me.

"You can't be annoyed!" Wren called.

"Why not?" I replied.

"Because I'm annoyed."

"So, we can't both be annoyed?"

She appeared at the top of the stairs. "No."

"Why not?" This conversation was making me more annoyed.

"Don't take that tone with me."

"I thought we were staying out of each other's heads?" I said with a frown.

"I can't help it! My hormones are going haywire and the baby is kicking and I'm tired and I'm hungry but I'm so sick of apples but they're the only thing I want and I can't stop dreaming about this damned cupid and I'm just!" She yelled unintelligibly. "I just want my husband to hold me and tell me everything's fine and let me cry or yell or whatever!"

"I didn't ask you to get pregnant," I snapped, knowing it wasn't fair to be angry with her but doing it anyway.

"Excuse me?"

"You're excused." I started up the stairs.

"What the hell is your problem?"

The last word ended of a yell as she pointed at me and I was blasted backwards with a power I was pretty sure the baby wasn't supposed to have. It wasn't a power I had.

I crashed into the wall behind me and the air rushed out of my body.

"Oh shit!" Wren cried and hurried down the stairs to drop next to me. "What did I do? Are you okay?"

Her hands fluttered uselessly over me, but I appreciated the concern. I grunted as I pulled myself to a more dignified sit.

"I think I'm okay," I told her.

"Are you sure? Did I break anything? How did I even do that?"

I grabbed her wrists to stop her hands hovering. "Just… Deep breath, love," I said softly.

She took a deep breath and looked at me. "You're okay?"

"Winded, but fine. Cadriel gives me worse every day."

She sighed in relief. "What had you storming in here like that?" she asked.

I stretched my neck and coaxed her and her growing belly into my lap nice and awkwardly. I wrapped my arms around her and she rested her head on my shoulder.

"Dad just told me he wasn't responsible for Mum's death. Not really."

"What? How?"

I told her what he'd told me. Saying it out loud helped me process it, helped me feel less helpless in the face of it.

"You're not going after him, are you?" she asked me.

I shook my head then leant it on hers. "Not now. There's a strong risk he'd beat me – supernova or no – and I couldn't do that to you or the baby."

I put my hand on her belly and she lay hers over mine.

"Our child won't suffer your same fate, Drake."

I could only nod as I held her closer. I couldn't imagine what I'd do if I lost her. I didn't know what I'd do if we lost the baby. I couldn't picture a world where that possibility existed.

But the fact was, strange powers or not, that her human body might not have the power to survive the rest of the pregnancy or the birth.

12

Wren

Lucifer hadn't known what to make of me blasting Drake down the stairs. Or, if he did, he didn't tell us. His only going theory was that the baby had some fancy powers no other Nephilim had.

As far as excuses went, I wasn't totally convinced. Lucifer had outright said he didn't know how or why that power had manifested in me. But that was a very different thing to him having a fairly well-educated guess and keeping it to himself.

What he had decided to do though was have a party.

And this one wasn't one of his usual Hell parties. He said he'd wanted to have the in-laws and Harmony down as a matter of courtesy, say hello, do some bonding.

Originally, I hadn't really seen the sense in having them wander around Hell and potentially get lost, or accidentally tortured, or eat or drink something that would get them stuck there a quarter of the year.

Lucifer and Truman both assured me that it was possible to feed people food not of Hell when they came for a visit. And it was a good thing that this was what Truman had done on previous visits because I hadn't thought about it at the time.

So, we were all decked out like we were going to a garden party and going to meet my family and Harmony in the throne room. Nerves ate me up on the way.

My father-in-law had told me he wasn't doing the traditional Hell party, but his idea of what wasn't a Hell party could easily have differed from mine. He could still have ghost waiters, or those demons with the penises all over their bodies pouring the wine.

I envisioned a hundred terrible scenarios on our walk. With each one, I knew my family would have expected something awful anyway, and Harmony would have cared even less. But that didn't really make me feel any better. And it made me feel more guilty for hoping for one night of normalcy in the outrageousness my life had become. I didn't regret any decision I'd made to lead me to where I was, I just didn't think it would hurt to feel human again for a little bit.

Which is why I was so surprised – and pleasantly so – when we walked into the throne room and found it looked exactly like a garden party out of a movie.

There was grass underfoot. The walls were lined with trees, giving the illusion that they went on for miles and we were surrounded by forest. Fairy lights hung across the ceiling.

There were small tables surrounded by chairs dotted around the place. And there were flowers, tables of food and drink, and an actual string quartet. It was all pastels and the sort of party where you drink too much bubbly, throw up in a bush and hope no one notices.

"This isn't very Hellish," I said to Drake.

"I think my father's missing Earth a little," he chuckled roughly.

My family were already there, as was Harmony. Even God made an appearance, though Lucifer was ignoring him stoically.

We did the round of greetings, caught everyone up on every minute of the pregnancy we could remember since we last saw them, and finally got around to eating when Harmony announce that, "The pregnant woman is starving."

We sectioned off into smaller groups and it was lovely to have a quieter catch up with people.

Lucifer made sure to dance with Mum, Tilly and Harmony. He even managed to persuade Dad to get up for a few minutes. But, after stepping on Lucifer's toes one too many times, even Lucifer gave up on redeeming his dance skill – or lack thereof.

"You're looking well, darling," Mum said.

I nodded. "I feel well. Aside from the whole being unable to lose my temper or I risk breaking everything in the house, I feel good."

"Kicking much?"

I nodded. "Little bit."

"So, your father's hopes of it playing AFL aren't coming true yet?"

I laughed. "No. No sign of that. I'll be sure to let him know if anything changes, though."

I decided not to remind her that the kid was being brought up in Hell. I was pretty sure that being able to proudly say it was morally ambiguous was about as glowing a report as I was going to be able to give to humans. And morally ambiguous probably didn't really have a place in organised sports.

Later on, I found myself standing with Harmony next to the food table.

"Are you sure this is okay for me to eat?" she asked, holding it up. "I trust food at your house. But eating in the literal hall of the devil seems like a recipe for trickery."

I nodded as I stuffed yet another slice of apple tea cake into my mouth. "He gave me his word. Truman gave me his word. Drake gave me his word. I would be the only live mortal in Hell to be 'tricked' into staying."

I used quotations there because I wasn't sure if I could really call myself tricked when I didn't know it was possible to be tricked in the first place.

"Good. Because I love you and I'm all for seeing you as often as I can. But I'm not sure I can do three months of Earth time here a year. That's just insanity."

I caught Persephone's eye and wondered how she'd felt about it. She'd obviously been doing everything she could to not end up with Lucifer and had had her parents make him compromise for the time she spent in the underworld. But there were times she honestly didn't seem to mind and actually maybe loved him.

"I doubt Lucifer needs any more mortals running around Hell that he needs to make sure don't fall in the Lethe or get eaten by Cerberus."

"Mortals," she chuckled. "Oh hey, speaking of things that aren't mortal–"

"We're not really, but okay."

"Have you seen Thane lately?"

I snuck a look at her and found her avoiding my gaze. "I might have. Why? You interested?"

"Just interested in if you've seen a mutual friend of ours recently," she answered coyly.

I snorted, then sobered fast.

I thought I'd caught something out of the corner of my eye. I turned quickly but, whatever I'd thought it was, there was nothing there but the other party guests.

"You okay?" Harmony asked.

I nodded, but my eyes were still scanning the room.

I smelled lavender and frangipani. I felt the breeze soft on my skin, somehow cooling in the depths of Hell.

Another glimpse from the corner of my eye and I whirled. I was sure Aksel would be there. But, again, nothing.

"Wren?"

I waved her concerns away, feeling something calling to me deeper than I'd felt the call of the Lethe.

"Serenity?" Harmony shook me gently and I turned back to her.

"What?" I asked, blinking.

"What did you see?"

"Nothing."

Because I hadn't. Not really.

Aksel had invaded my dreams apparently to the point I was seeing him when I was awake. That wasn't good.

I looked over to where Drake was talking to Persephone. He was already looking at me. His face was dark and I knew he knew what was going on in my head. I felt so guilty and weird about it that I didn't even mind he'd been in my head.

I knew I had nothing to feel guilty for, and I was sure Drake didn't blame me, but that didn't really make the feeling go away.

"Wren," Harmony said again. "You sure you're okay?"

"Uh…" I started. "You know what? I'm actually not feeling great. I think I need to go have a lie down."

I had no intention of lying down. Not when it risked me dreaming about Aksel again.

"No worries. I'll talk to you later?"

I nodded absently. "Get home safe, yeah?"

We hugged and I hurried out.

Drake caught me not that far out of the throne room.

"What happened?" he asked.

I shrugged. "I don't know. I thought I saw Aksel. Like in the flesh, at your dad's party, saw Aksel."

Drake frowned and looked around as though he was going to see him as well.

"A cupid wouldn't be stupid enough to enter Hell," Drake muttered, but more like he was reassuring himself.

"I didn't think he would. So why did I see him?"

Drake's eyes came back to me and he looked me over. "Cupid's are crafty bastards. They're inherently love personified. Or deified. If they do their job wrong, the mortal falls for them."

I blinked, not quite sure what that meant for me.

"It means you're being pursued by a cupid and we don't know why. And if you're not careful, I'll lose you to him because he's obviously doing his job wrong."

"But I love you."

He nodded. "I know."

"So, can I fall in love with a cupid if I'm already in love."

"Falling for a cupid isn't love, Wren. It's pure, unabashed obsession plain and simple. Similar to the fae, but more dangerous."

"More dangerous how?"

"Because instead of wasting away for love of a fae, you'll kill yourself for love of a cupid."

"I'll do what?"

"Cupids are angels. Somehow mortals get it into their heads that they kill themselves and they'll get to be with the cupid."

"But suicide gets you–"

"To Hell. I didn't say it made sense. Obsession is blinding. And cupids have no feelings."

"They… Sorry, what?"

Drake nodded. "I know it sounds weird, but they don't have feelings. They're built to facilitate love, but they don't feel it. They're cold bastards who don't give a fuck for one more mortal shuffling off the coil."

I tried to lighten the mood. "But if I kill myself, I'll just end up back with you." I failed.

He frowned. "Killing our child in the process and who knows what state you'll be in. Can you just not fall for him in the first place?"

I nodded. "I can do that."

"Are you sure?"

I nodded again. "Yes. I'm sure."

"Okay."

"What are we going to do in the meantime?"

"What do you mean?"

"Well, are we just going to sit back while a cupid pursues me?" I asked.

His smirk was sexy and wry. "Fuck, but you're my wife, all right."

I smiled at him. "I'm learning."

"I'll talk to Cadriel."

"And until then?"

I knew he'd caught the thought running through my mind because his smirk was back in full force. "Until then, I know just how to keep you occupied and not thinking about wanker cupids."

Drake took me home and followed through on every promise so well that, if I dreamt about Aksel again, I didn't remember it the next day.

Drake

I was beyond angry and it was getting harder to hide it. Thankfully, I didn't have to hide it with Cadriel.

"For fuck's sake!" he snapped and he wrenched out of my grip, leaving a few feathers behind in my hand. "What have I said about the wings?"

"Do I look like I care?" I raged.

"This is shit," he said matter-of-fact as he whipped his axe up to block my strike.

"What is?" I huffed, swinging again.

"This cupid bullshit. You're not even close to supernova."

"Don't fucking bring up supernova again, you giant twat," I grumbled.

The last thing I needed was a reminder of losing Wren, which is all that the idea of supernova ever did for me anymore.

"Perhaps I bring it up because it's important."

"Perhaps you bring it up because you think you've got a few too many feathers left."

As though to make a point, Cadriel retracted his wings. "My point is, you might be worried about her, but you're not worried about her drying."

I scoffed, "Yeah. Until she falls for the cupid arsehole and kills herself to be with him."

"Your baby might be born by then?" he suggested and I yelled at him as I swung for his neck.

Unfortunately, I failed to decapitate him.

"What I am trying to get your half-Neanderthal brain to realise is that you still think there's hope."

I paused and his axe head crashed into me. I was saved lucky it hadn't been one of the bladed edges.

"Ow," I said pointedly.

"How many times do I have to tell you to pay attention? Honestly, it's like you're thirteen again and obsessed with those succubi."

"Yeah, yeah. You hate everything. Go back to the hope bit."

Cadriel shrugged. "What?"

"Why do you think I have hope?"

"Because you only go supernova when you think you're going to lose her. You're pissed enough to wake fucking Ra at this point, but there is no hint of supernova. Ergo…?"

"I know the fight's not over."

Cadriel nodded and gave an exaggerated bow. "Now do you feel like ripping all my feathers out?"

"Yes."

"What? Why?"

"Because that's not an answer to anything but why I haven't caused a cave-in. How do I win the fight?"

Cadriel leant on his axe, just the way all good mortal instructors would tell you not to.

"Short of getting a baku to deal with the dreams, I'm not sure what we could do," I said.

"How about we just don't let her sleep?"

"She's pregnant, she can't not sleep."

"Send her to Earth?"

A chill ran up my spine and I couldn't believe I was considering it. There were so many variables and so many risks that it was surely not worth it. But then, what was stronger than a cupid's pride and vanity?

"What?" Cadriel asked. "I know that face. That's your 'I've got an idea' face."

"It's an awful idea," I admitted.

He shrugged. "So? I have something like ten awful ideas just before breakfast."

I frowned at him. "We puff his pride."

Cadriel tapped his chin. "Okay. Okay. I think I see where you're going here."

"We send her to Earth for a bit. Get Dad on board. And we puff up his holy ego."

"Make him think she's subconsciously looking for him. Draw him out."

I nodded. "Exactly. Lull him into a sweet false sense of security."

"Then cut his fucking head off!"

I started nodding, then stopped. "No. We can't go up."

Cadriel's glee turned sour. "You're right. If we go as well, then how will we have the moral high ground when it's discovered a cupid was on Earth during the embargo?" he said, completely deadpan and mostly taking the mickey.

"I'm thinking further than that."

Cadriel's glee was back. "You want to lure him here."

I nodded. "I do."

"If he trespasses in Hell on unofficial business and we happen to kill him, we don't get in an unnecessary trouble."

"And the message is sent to the cupids."

"What I still don't get is why they're after her anyway."

I shrugged. "I don't know either."

"I've got to wonder if it is the clean-up. I mean she's a loose end. She's not dead, but she lives in Hell. She belongs in Hell but is mortal. She could end up being some kind of goddess or saint or something to the humans."

"And Michael couldn't very well have that. He'd be out of a job."

"Fucking brown-noser. Your grandfather doesn't even care what creation does anymore. There'll always be some version of him somewhere, enough to keep him going. I don't know why Michael's so bothered with staying relevant."

"World we live in, I guess."

Cadriel nodded. "You're not wrong though. Speaking of your beautiful wife, has she thrown you across a room again recently?" he sniggered.

I could still feel the bruised bone from mere hours ago. "It seems like a power that's hanging around for a while."

Cadriel swung his axe back up. "I don't envy you, Morningstar. A mortal with the powers of a celestial? I remember when you were coming into your powers. Fucking hilarious. The shit you got up to."

I smiled. "I'm glad you enjoyed it. I don't know how many other beings did."

Cadriel shrugged, then quickly threw his axe up to block my blow. "I don't really care what anyone else thought about it."

"You're always out for number one, Grigori."

"After your god lets you down, it really does a number on your ability to put faith in anyone else."

"I suppose I'm lucky I never really had much faith in God in the first place, aren't I?"

It had only taken me a few months in Hell before I started to wonder if Mum hadn't practiced any organised religion because she knew everything about it. To say she knew it was a crock of shit was going a bit far. But if she knew my father was the literal Devil, then perhaps she had her doubts about the other figures of mythology as well.

"He wins you over in the end," Cadriel said. "If only to break your heart to pieces at the end of it."

"You make him sound heartless."

"Have you met the Jews?"

I smirked. "Fair point."

"Enough talk about distressing and boring things. More fighting."

I couldn't argue with that.

I had no idea if my idea for trying to flush the cupid out was going to work. I was grown up enough to admit I was afraid that I'd lose Wren. But she'd promised she could resist the cupid. If a chance at saving her meant trusting her, then that was what I was going to do.

And I was going to find out why a cupid was pursuing my wife before I ripped his wings out by the roots and impaled him with them.

Wren

Despite the embargo on Earth, Lucifer had convinced God that it would be good for me get some fresh Earth air for the baby. And, given that I was still technically mortal, I wasn't technically disobeying the embargo.

I'd stood outside Harmony's door and just breathed in deeply. The air was different after the months I'd been in Hell. Of course, it had only been weeks on Earth. So, it was still summer in Australia, which was hardly better than Hell really.

But where was the best place to go in an Australian summer? The Plaza. Miles of undercover shopping and all perfectly air conditioned.

"Remind me to hang out in Hell when I'm pregnant," Harmony said as we walked along happily aimlessly.

"Are you planning on being pregnant any time soon?" I asked, my eyebrow rising.

Harmony actually blushed a little. "No."

"No?" I laughed. "Very convincing."

"I'm not!" she insisted.

"Of course, not. You're just thinking about it."

She shrugged. "I've thought about it."

"Does this have anything to do with a certain entity? Long black robes, fond of farm equipment, little pale?"

By her smile, I knew my guess was right.

"Nothing's happened," she said definitely.

"But you want something to happen?"

She gave me a coy glance. "I don't know. Maybe. What do you think?"

"I think he's super not my type, but I'm not going to stand in the way of my best friend and Death."

She laughed. "Oh, God. Don't say it like that!"

"Sorry. You know what I meant."

She nodded. "I do. And, I didn't think he was my type either. But… I dunno. I feel like there's something there. A connection?"

"Let out your inner Dickinson and have yourself an affair with Death," I told her.

"See, it sounds *way* better when you put it like that. Why didn't you put it like that the first time?"

I grinned. "Because where would the fun be in that?"

Harmony looked around. "No guards today?"

"The embargo. I'm strictly not supposed to be here. Sort of. A guard would have been a right tip off."

"Lemme just ask. What happens if one side or the other disobeys the embargo? Like, does the world implode? Apocalypse actual now?"

I thought about it for a moment. "I honestly don't know. I know there's a Michael guy. He sounds really bossy and sounds like he has as many Daddy issues as Lucifer and Drake combined."

"Damn," Harmony snorted. "Does Thane have a father by chance? Asking for a friend."

"Worried about getting caught in those Daddy issues?"

"Something like that."

I shrugged. "I don't think so. I don't know a lot about him, but then I've heard he doesn't know a lot about him either."

"How does he not know a lot about him?"

"Drake said he's as old or older than God or Lucifer. He doesn't know much about how he began I guess."

"Hm," Harmony mused. "I guess if you asked God or Lucifer how they came to be, they might not remember either."

I nodded. "True."

"Oh, hey." She pointed to a shop. "There is a sale that is begging to take all my money."

I laughed and we headed inside.

Harmony started pulling things off racks and asking my opinion. As usual, everything she was looking at would suit her amazingly – she just had one of those bodies that everything just seemed to fit. Normally, it didn't bother me, but I was feeling a touch self-conscious being a teen pregnancy at the shops.

I knew people didn't know me and I had a wedding ring on. But that stuff shouldn't matter and, to the people it mattered to, it didn't stop them making judgements anyway.

And it wasn't just the sudden reminder of how I really didn't fit into this world anymore – because, let's face it, I was going to look like a teenager anytime I came to visit for the foreseeable future if not forever. It was also because I didn't feel like trying clothes on over my baby bump. Nothing would fit and I couldn't be bothered arguing with Harmony about how I still looked cute anyway.

So, while she was in the changerooms, I wandered.

I had no particular spot in mind, I was just meandering around the shop. I filed some things away for later to mention to her in case what she hadn't picked out yet counted as enough.

When I blinked and realised I was standing in the middle of the indoor garden, I was slightly confused. I'd heard the term 'baby brain', but that had to be ridiculous. Surely it didn't make you forget you'd walked across half the mall.

I wasn't worried about 'baby brain' or anything else for very long, though.

A masculine figure materialised out of the shadows and stalked towards me. He was wearing plain jeans and a t-shirt.

Nothing fancy. But he didn't need anything, he was the decoration.

I stepped towards him, on auto-pilot. He held his hand out and I took it. We stepped closer, until we were only half a foot apart.

If I'd thought he was intoxicating in my dreams, he was even more so in real life. I felt heady, like I'd drunk too much of Alexander's favourite wine, only it hadn't left a weird taste in my mouth.

"How did you get to Earth?" he asked, drawing me closer.

I fought to resist him. I knew I didn't want him. I knew all I wanted was Drake. But it was like I was locked out of my own brain. I didn't control my thoughts, my feelings, or my body anymore. Because everything was filling with Aksel.

He dropped his nose to my neck and I felt goose bumps break out along my skin.

"How did you get to Earth?" he asked again, his voice low and seductive.

I opened my mouth to tell him I didn't know what he was talking about, but couldn't form the words.

I opened my mouth to tell him I found a door all by myself, but couldn't find the words.

I opened my mouth to say I found my own way, and almost got the words out.

But what came out instead was, "How did *you* get to Earth? I thought both sides had to obey the embargo? I don't imagine a cupid is the bare minimum needed to keep the ship running."

I felt his smile in the movement of his cheek against mine. "You *are* the wife of the Morningstar's son."

"You go about seducing random women in the hope of meeting me often?" I asked, pulling away from him.

His smile fair blew me away. The guy was perfection itself. Like he was taken from the base daydreams of every human and carved to be everyone's perfect mate.

It had to be some kind of magic.

Drake had said their effect on humans was like humans to Grigori – or, for a slightly less celestial option, like catnip to a cat. Well, I was feeling it.

He was nigh irresistible. I couldn't even form the words for what I wanted him to do to me, I was so lost in a drunken haze of desire. I felt as though my whole world would crumble if I didn't spend every minute of the rest of my life with him.

"I can protect you, Serenity," he said.

"Protect me from what?" I asked.

"From those that would do you harm, would do your child harm."

Something felt off, but only in that locked-out part of my brain that was fighting for control.

"Why would anyone want to do me harm?"

He lay his hand on my stomach protectively. "Your child is special. You want it to be raised properly, don't you? Without fear and hate. You want it to be good?"

I nodded. "Of course. Don't all mothers want that for their children?"

"I can give your child that, Serenity. Can the Nephilim say the same?"

I pulled away to look at him. "Drake will be an excellent father."

"Do you really believe that? Or do you feel you have no choice? You have a choice. You can choose me."

Aksel took my chin in his hand and tilted my face towards him as he leant down to meet me. My heart pounded in my chest. Just as our lips were about to touch, I freed myself.

I took a hurried step away from him, pulling out of his grasp.

"I have to go," I said, annoyed with how breathless I sounded.

I turned and practically ran back to Harmony. She saw the frazzled look on my face and didn't ask questions. Her purchases were left forgotten and we went straight home.

Drake

Only time would tell if the plan had worked.

Dad, of course, had jumped right on board any excuse to mess with an angel, even if that had meant risking Wren. But she'd come home safe to us and other than an almost-kiss I pretended I hadn't seen in her mind, she'd resisted the temptation of the cupid.

While I was pissed that she'd almost kissed that arsehole, I knew it wasn't her fault. And I was more than gratified that she'd managed to pull away in time. I was also very pleased that the cupid was likely to be bolder now.

He'd almost got what he wanted – for whatever reason he wanted it – he wasn't likely to give up now. Cupids, like all angels, were arrogant sods who firmly believed that the world was owed to them and then some. They couldn't fathom that someone would be smart enough to lay a trap for them, or work out what they were doing in order to stop them.

So, it was only a matter of time until he turned up in Hell. There were enough creatures in there that you could turn to your cause in order to get some alone time with Lucifer's daughter-in-law, after all.

Until then, we played the waiting game.

Not that any of us were very good at it.

"I hear Wren got home unscathed," Dad said while we were sitting in front of the totally unnecessary fire one evening.

He'd declared we needed some father-son time and cleared everyone out for as long as he saw fit.

I nodded. "In and out. As far as Cadriel can tell, Michael was none the wiser."

"And the cupid?"

"Baited. We just have to see if he bites now."

"Exactly how have you kept this from Wren when she can read your mind?"

I swished my brandy balloon. "Miraculously, obviously."

"Is she losing her powers?"

I shook my head and held up my arm. "This still healing gash would suggest not."

"What did she do?"

"She was pointing for me to pass her a mug and accidentally threw the marble table into me."

Dad nodded. "Ah, yes. Accidentally. Lets one get away with a multitude of sins, doesn't it?"

I smirked, but there wasn't a lot of humour in it. "In Wren's case, it actually was an accident. She ended up blasting me through the French doors in her attempt to stop the table hitting me."

"That's powerful."

"It's useless if she doesn't get a handle on it."

"It's not like it took you overnight to figure out your powers," he reminded me.

I nodded thoughtfully.

"Go on. Spit it out," he encouraged.

I looked at him and wondered if I had the energy and the affection to do what could only be described as bonding. He was my father after all. Maybe not a great one, but he was the only one I had.

"Thanks," he huffed, but he smiled ruefully.

"How will the baby's powers work?"

"Much like yours. What do you mean?"

"As in, will it be able to use them sooner? Later? Will it just be a pregnancy thing and Wren and the baby will both be powerless mortals once it's born?"

"For starts, Wren has never nor will she ever be a powerless mortal. She's got brains on her and a wit as I've ever seen. She'll be fine, 'divine powers' or not. As for the baby, I don't know."

I sighed. "I know every Nephilim is different."

He nodded. "That it is. Some are incredibly powerful, some aren't. Weirdly, it doesn't seem to matter how powerful the angelic parent."

"We you worried?"

"About your powers? No. I always knew you'd shine brightly, as a Morningstar should."

"No. I meant about being a parent."

"I've never had the luxury to worry about being a parent, Drake. When I first had children, I was arrogant enough to think I knew everything. Now I know I know almost everything, I realise I've never really bothered trying to parent. And I realise I have failed you the most."

"You haven't…failed me."

"No? What would you call it? The Morningstar men just have a different idea of what parenting looks like?"

"I'm alive–"

"Very little thanks go to me for that one."

"I have enough job satisfaction–"

"That's nature, not nurture."

"And I'm happily married with a child on the way."

"Ah, now. That one was all me."

I looked at him pointedly.

"All right. Not *all* me, I suppose. You got her pregnant. But it's because of my meddling you had the chance to do that."

I nodded. "I'm honestly not sure if I should thump you or thank you."

146

"Are you that worried about becoming a parent?"

I looked into the flames as though I wasn't surrounded by them on a daily basis. And, even though I was, I still found them incredibly beautiful.

"When we were on our honeymoon, I yearned for the normalcy of a human life. At least in part," I amended quickly. "I wanted the house, the dog, the two point five children and the picket fence."

"I'd like to point out that I think Wren would look unfavourably on cutting one child in half…"

I gave him a small smile. "I honestly thought we could have a normal life. Then we got back and things were… I was back to work and we settled into this routine that worked for us. We were happy."

"Then came the next big change."

"I just don't want to mess it up."

"The kid is going to grow up in Hell, trailing after Kyle and his mandagot all day. Or, if not Kyle, Ignacio and learning about bombs or carving names in skin. Cadriel's going to have it swinging a blade before it can walk. You can't mess a kid up any more than that, and that's normal for us, son."

He had a point. A Hellish upbringing ensured that, by most being's standards on parenting, it wasn't going to be 'well adjusted'. As long as it knew I cared for it, how much more harm could I really do?

"Was I actually helpful for once?" Dad asked with a smirk.

I hid my return smile in my brandy glass. "Perhaps."

"The execution might remain unpractised, but I understand the theory well enough."

"Have you ever thought about more kids?"

"At my age?" Dad laughed.

"You're immortal. Age is irrelevant."

Dad wriggled in his seat like he was suddenly uncomfortable. "Not the way you're thinking, son."

"Why not?"

"Because there comes a time in a man's life when he's tired of watching the women he loves dying either to bring his children into the world or protecting those children later on. Immortality." He paused and looked at me. "True immortality is more than just being able to fight with Fallen and not die. It is more than eons lived in the underworld."

"So, you do feel love then?"

Dad looked at me almost surprised. "Of course, I do."

"I've always wondered what Mum was to you."

"She was a remarkable woman. I should have resisted. I should have walked away. But I told myself it was harmless. It was the age of near-infallible birth control. If there was ever a time to truly love a woman, no holding back and without fears, it was then."

"And that obviously backfired."

"It is what it is."

"Did you want nothing to do with me, or did she push you away?"

"Bit of both, not really either. Your life was in jeopardy the moment you were born. I naively – stupidly – thought that you'd be safer without me. And it worked for a time."

"But not forever."

Dad sighed. "Not forever, Drake. Nothing truly lasts forever."

It wasn't the advice I wanted. I didn't want to consider the possibility that Wren and I might not last until the end days. I firmly believed that we were made to last the distance. I could hardly even imagine the rest of time before her. Now, the rest of time didn't seem long enough to have with her.

But I knew it was the advice I needed.

I had to be prepared. I had to be prepared to lose Wren. I had to be prepared to lose our child. I had to be prepared to lose the devilbums. I'd even feel something if I lost Cadriel.

"Loss does not always mean death," Dad said quietly. "Often the worst loss is when they're just out of reach."

Wren

The last few weeks had been getting harder and harder. I was more irritable. I was more tired. I'd started setting things on fire. Kyle's poor mandagot had its tale set on fire twice that week alone.

I reminded myself on an hourly basis that it was all worth it, that I was lucky to be pregnant in the first place. And, for the most part, I was thankful and I knew it was worth it. Then I'd get a swift kick to the kidneys and forget for a moment – at least it looked more like Dad was going to get his AFL player.

The only good thing to come out of it was that I was having less dreams about Aksel. They were more intense, but they were fewer and I chose to see that as a win.

To avoid them, I hadn't been sleeping properly and I'd felt my strength waning considerably in the previous week particularly. The baby felt huge – even though I still had a couple of months to go – and wriggly. It was so restless. Every time it moved, it felt like it was literally draining me of energy.

I supposed that was probably how most Nephilim mothers ended up dying. Maybe the baby really did just leech all their energy.

Everyone had put me on rest and the boys were doing their utmost to make sure I had everything I might want.

"Is this how it happens?" I asked Truman as he brought me a cup of tea where I was rugged up on the couch.

"How what happens, ma'am?" he asked.

"Baby and mother dying."

Truman plopped onto the other couch and looked at me. "In what way?"

"Does the baby leech my energy to the point it kills us both?"

Truman cocked his head slightly. "Sort of, I suppose. A mortal body was never intended to carry angelic offspring, no matter how pure or dilute. Thus, when a mortal is carrying angelic offspring, it takes more out of the mortal. Even Nephilim are half celestial, ma'am. Mortal bodies weren't built to contain celestial power."

"Is my baby killing me, Truman?" I asked him.

He sighed. "I don't rightly know, ma'am. I believe in you. You're a fighter, through and through. You've shown that more than once. But I'm not sure sheer force of will can get you through this."

If anything was going to get me through it, all I had was sheer force of will.

"What's your educated opinion?"

"That you may not be with us much longer, ma'am."

I took a deep breath and nodded. "All right then."

So, I made the most of it. I hung on as long as I could while I tried to force myself not to give up. Truman had said he didn't think sheer force of will was going to do it. Well, I wasn't going out with a fight.

Then, one day, something happened.

There was a twinge in my stomach. It felt like it jolted out from the baby and shot through my body. My heart literally stopped for a moment. I gasped for breath as I sat forward.

"Ma'am?" Truman asked.

I could only shake my head and it felt like I was suffocating from the inside. My vision swam.

I just managed a croaked, "Lucifer," before energy zinged through me like every nerve was lit up.

"Wren?" I heard Lucifer say as he dropped beside me.

I could only open and close my mouth as I looked at him. I saw the question in his eyes before his lips, but he didn't get a chance to ask it.

Because, just then, my heart restarted. I wasn't sure if it pounded harder or if it just felt that way after the absence of its steady beat.

"What happened?" I gasped.

Lucifer looked me over. Forcing my eyes open.

"Wren, look at me," he commanded. "Look at me properly."

I did my best approximation of looking at him properly.

"Truman, what happened?"

"She just sat up, then it was like she couldn't breathe, her heart stopped, then you arrived and her eyes glowed."

"My eyes glowed?" I asked.

Drake had said once that he'd thought my eyes had glowed but he must have been imagining it.

Lucifer nodded. "They're glowing now."

"What happened?" Drake said as he dropped through the house. His wings were folded before he dropped to my side. "What happened? Are you okay? Is the baby okay?"

"They're both fine, Drake," Lucifer said. His tone sounded somewhat awed, but I wasn't really concentrating on that just then.

"Fine? She doesn't look fine. Her eyes are glowing. Why are her eyes glowing?"

Drake fussed over me while Lucifer sat in silence for what felt like the longest time. Finally, Drake seemed happy enough that was indeed okay and turned to his father.

"What's going on?"

"I never even imagined," Lucifer breathed.

I wriggled in a vain attempt to get comfortable. "Imagined what?"

"I didn't think he'd do it. It's been centuries. Millennia."

"Who? What has?" Drake asked.

"The reason Wren's survived. The powers she has that no Nephilim has ever been known to have." Lucifer looked at me again like a precious commodity. "She's celestial."

"Wait. What?" I looked around, not believing for a single second that that could even begin to be true. "I'm what? How?"

"Grandad is the only one powerful enough to bestow Celestial status on a mortal, isn't he?"

Lucifer frowned. "These days, yes."

Again, I actively decided not to overthink the whole different mythos thing.

"Is that why I'm not dead yet?"

Lucifer nodded. "That is the only reason you're not dead and the only reason you will not die. The baby is no half-half now. Instead of being three parts human and one part angelic, your child is now three parts angelic and one part human."

I didn't care to ask how he knew that.

"Is that…bad?" I asked uncertainly.

"I wouldn't say bad, no. I'm not aware there has ever been a baby born who was more than half angelic. It's been, hitherto, impossible. There have been no female angels."

"Until now?" Drake asked.

Lucifer's expression was noncommittal. "Wren's not exactly angel…"

"What is she then?"

"Closest approximation I can come to is lower goddess."

"Not very Christian of Grandad."

Lucifer grinned. "He wasn't always a Christian god."

I tried, and failed, to sit up. "Why did he do this?"

"Don't look a gift horse in the mouth," Lucifer said. "That way lies Trojans." His nose wrinkled. "I have *never* understood that. Wouldn't you *want* the warning about the Trojans?" He shook his head. "Anyway. My point is that the Almighty Lord of the Sky does what he wants when he wants. If he wanted to make you celestial so his great-grandchild didn't kill you, don't question it. Just send him a gift basket in thanks."

I lifted my hand and looked at it. For some reason, I was expecting it to look different. I didn't know what I expected to see. Sparks playing along my fingers maybe. My veins glowing as though that would prove the power running through them. Maybe I was expecting them to be a different colour.

Whatever I was expecting, it looked the same as it always did. But of course it did. Drake looked, for all intents and purposes, human. The only times he didn't were when his eyes glowed red or his wings sprouted.

I lifted my hand to my cheek. My eyes felt hot. Not as though I was about to cry hot, just warm. More like when you close your eyes against a cold wind and they feel warm again.

"Does this mean she's going to be okay?" Drake asked.

Lucifer nodded. "She's going to be more than okay. Her and the baby both."

But, just at that moment, I only had one question. "Does this mean I'm going to get wings?"

Lucifer smiled and I could tell Drake's laugh was more relief than humour.

"We shall see, Wren," Lucifer answered. "We shall see."

17

Drake

We didn't have much longer before the baby was born, provided it stuck to normal gestation periods and Persephone and Dad weren't wrong about the due date.

I'd stopped worrying about Wren. In the last few weeks since we discovered she'd become celestial, she'd regained all her former strength and then some. The colour was back in her face and she was vibrant. It wasn't just a maternal glow that lit her up, but a divine one.

The only vaguely concerning thing was that there had been no appearance by Aksel and his influence on Wren's dreams seemed to be lessening by the week. I didn't know if it was her strength or if he was up to something. Knowing a cupid, it was a play – withdraw his 'love' so she grew desperate, then pop in at the very last second as though you're a knight in shining armour.

Sex was getting awkward and apparently our child wasn't a big fan of Mum and Dad having Mum and Dad time. So, we'd given up trying. Too many times she'd got a foot in an organ and twice I'd got a kick as well. It was like the little blighter knew what was going on and had inherited its cock blocking abilities from its grandfather.

Which made me think of something.

"Do you think the baby can read our minds?"

"I don't see why not," Wren answered as she turned the page of her book. "It seems a fairly strong genetic trait the Morningstars pass on."

"No," I said quietly. "I mean right now."

She turned enough to look at me and I could see she was barely suppressing the laughter. "Why? Are you thinking things you don't want it to know?"

"Not really. I just wonder how it knows whenever we try to get physical."

Wren leant back against me. "I don't know. Maybe it's got something to do with the fact that it recognises movements."

"How? I doubt it's got much idea about sex yet."

Wren laughed. "I don't know, Drake. Maybe it *can* read our minds."

We just sat together for a while, hands entwined while she read and I just enjoyed the moment.

Sex was definitely great. I wasn't going to say that I could give up sex for the rest of time. But I liked this. I liked just being with her. It was intimate, but on a different level. It was the times like these that I knew for certain that Wren was the one for me for eternity. If I could sit with her and do nothing and not feel like eviscerating something, then it must be love.

"Have you thought about names?" I asked her.

She lay her book down. It wasn't the exasperated way she sometimes did. It was just to concentrate on the conversation.

"I guess not really. We've never really talked about it, so I guess I haven't thought about it much."

I felt guilty and I wasn't sure if I was supposed to or not.

"Did you want to?"

"Want to want?"

"Talk about it?"

I felt her smile against my arm. "Do you want to talk about it?"

I shrugged gently. "I have nothing against talking about it."

"That's not a yes."

I kissed her hair. "If you want to, yes. If you don't, no."

"Do you want a girl or a boy?" she asked.

"Am I supposed to have a preference?" I asked.

"I don't know. I've never done this before."

I wrapped my arm around her with a smile. "Very cute. Do you have a preference?"

She shook her head and lay it on my arm. "I don't think so. I've heard terrible things about boys *and* girls."

"How about boys or girls with divine powers?"

"Surely the worst is worse?" she asked as she rolled her head to look at me.

I shrugged. "I don't know. Why are you looking at me?"

She smiled. "Because you were once a little boy with divine powers."

"How am I supposed to know if I was worse than mortal boys or not?"

She shrugged. "Don't know. Just thought you might have *some* idea."

"Sorry. I've got nothing."

"Do you have any family names?"

"Jesus seems popular in certain parts of the world."

She snorted. "How about we put it in the maybe pile?"

"Beings in my family seem to live too long for names to really be passed on. It'd be confusing if you just had a bunch of Lucifers and Michaels running around. Have you got any family names?"

She shook her head again. "Not that I can think of. The most uniform name we had was our last name."

I smiled softly, thinking there were worse names than Shaw if it was a boy.

"Shaw could be a boy or a girl."

I nodded, not even feeling the need to gently remind her to stay out of my head. "It could, at that."

"But doesn't that feel super narcissistic to call our kid my maiden name?"

"Why? They used to do it in the Georgian Era all the time."

"And how do you know that?"

I shrugged, holding her close. "I'm sure I've tortured a guy who had his mother's maiden name as his first name."

"Shaw Morningstar," she mused.

"I've heard worse names."

"You don't sound enamoured with it or anything."

"I think I'm just having trouble reconciling the fact that the thing in your stomach will soon be an actual being and we have to pick a name for it. I feel a bit detached and…"

"Like it's not real yet?" she finished.

"Just like that."

"I get it. I feel like that, too. And I'm so stressed that I'm going to be an awful mum. I'll drop it on its head or set it on fire. If these powers are a me thing not an it thing, I just don't want to hurt it."

"You won't."

"How do you know?"

"Because I know you. You're far too caring to let your powers get away from you and risk hurting our child."

"You don't know. That's just blind faith. And I thought you didn't do organised religion?"

I smirked. "Maybe you're my organised religion? I've certainly put in enough time worshipping at the temple of Wren for it."

She nestled further into me. "I don't think I can be an organised religion."

"Dad said you were a goddess now."

"A lower goddess. I don't think they have temples."

"Of course they do. How else do they exist?"

"Okay, maybe like a shrine."

"A shrine?"

She held her hand up with her finger and thumb almost touching. "Like a tiny shine."

"I hope that's describing a part of me."

She snorted. "I'm definitely not quick enough to have made a dick joke on purpose."

"Good. I'm not really sure I could handle that and divine powers."

"Can I get a refund on the divine powers, then?"

I laughed and hugged her tightly but gently. "I'll see if I can put in a word with Grandad."

"Thank you."

I kissed her again and rubbed my hand over her stomach.

Our child had a name, whether it turned out to be a boy or a girl. I supposed we could have found out, but no one had offered and I hadn't thought about it until then. But with only a few weeks – ish – left until it was born and eternity stretching beyond that, I felt like I could wait.

I just had to hope that whatever was happening with the cupids was over or would be sorted soon. When nothing happened over the next couple of weeks, I lulled myself into a sense of security, believing maybe he'd given up whatever it was they'd been trying to achieve.

But it was still a waiting game and only time would tell if it turned out to be false hope or not.

Wren

Everything seemed to be coming up Wren.

I was in no danger of being killed by my baby, even by accident when it was born and learning how to use its powers – something I hadn't even thought of until Ignacio helpfully pointed it out to me.

I was back helping with the baby devilbums. Pike in particular had missed me and had lots of things to show me when I got back.

As usual, I was avoiding Esther. But I felt like the feeling was mutual now. The only time we ever saw each other was at dinner and, even then, we ignored each other spectacularly.

And I still had regular lunch dates with Persephone. She seemed quite happy that it was almost time for the baby to be born, she just didn't want to say anything out loud.

I could tell Drake had stopped worrying as well. He seemed less hesitant to leave me on my own now. I wasn't sure if something brought it on and, even though we talked more now that sex was a little more awkward, I didn't want to bring it up and risk opening that can of worms all over again.

I was walking back from the hatchery, feeling like it must be pretty close to the baby's due date based on my waddling, when I felt the first breath of fresh breeze waft over me. It carried the scent of lavender and frangipani to my nose.

I looked around, but couldn't see anything.

Surely, Aksel wouldn't have got into Hell. Quite aside from the fact that I was sure the only was in was past Cerberus and there was no way the big three-headed dog was going to let a cupid in the place.

I passed a few demons I sort of knew by sight, but there were no other signs of Aksel except the tantalising breeze and the insistent urge to turn around. Not that I ignored it. I turned around, and often. There was just no one there.

I should have known that he'd ambush me in the darkest, quietest section of tunnel between the hatchery and home.

His hand slid into mine effortlessly and he turned me around to face him. My stomach felt like it had plummeted. My chest fluttered. I felt my hand closing tighter in his against my will. I was overcome with that weird heady feeling as I looked into his eyes.

It was almost enough to make me forget Drake, the baby in my womb, and everything I was making into a life for myself.

But I blinked and took a step back as something cleared my mind. I felt a self-satisfied smile grow on my face as Aksel looked at me in confusion.

"Let go of my wife," I heard Drake growl from behind me.

I turned to him, now the one confused. "What are you doing here?" I dimly registered that Aksel let go of my hand.

"It's cupid season," Cadriel said, seeming to solidify from the shadows. "We're hunting cupids."

"You're doing what?" I asked, incredulous.

"Leave this to us, Wren," Drake said, his eyes trained on the cupid.

"Drake, nothing happened," I said.

"You want me to spare this arsehole's life when he was pursuing you?"

I opened and closed my mouth, then shook my head. "Not really, no." I stepped out of the way and let my husband and Cadriel take over.

Had I not been pregnant, I would have tried to take Aksel out myself. As it was, I didn't want to risk anything unnecessarily. Drake and Cadriel would barely break a sweat against a single cupid out of his element. Surely.

But the fight wasn't fair.

Whereas Drake and Cadriel were trying to protect me and hurt Aksel, Aksel was just in the mood to hurt.

Both Drake and Cadriel were knocked to the side. Aksel lunged at me. He wrapped his arm around me and his pure white wings burst open.

I closed my eyes as we soared upwards.

The next thing I felt was tumbling. I opened my eyes just in time to see Drake catch me mid-flight. I looked around and saw Cadriel was driving Aksel back to the ground. And if their trajectory held, they were heading for a huge, bubbling crater.

"What's that?" I asked.

"The Hell Pit," Drake answered.

"Take us down."

"Wren–"

"Take us down, Drake."

He did as I asked and we alighted as Cadriel and Aksel kept fighting. I took my eyes off them long enough to look at the Hell Pit.

The only question I had to answer now was, was I strong enough?

As he turned, I grabbed hold of Aksel's throat and one of his flailing arms. With all the strength I didn't know I had, I drove him back towards the pit.

I held Aksel over the pit, feeling the fire from the depths of Hell whirl around us. My hair flew around my face and there was this weird heaviness at my back that seemed to counter-balance the almost nine-month belly at the front.

"How did you resist me?" he hissed, his mouth curled in a snarl.

"The same way this baby hasn't killed me yet, cupid," I told him.

His blue eyes went wide and I knew he'd understood. "How?" he asked.

I shrugged. "You don't need to know that."

"Only the Almighty can create celestials."

"Well, I guess you have to hope that there's reception where you're going so you can call him and ask him yourself."

He grabbed hold of the wrist of the hand holding his throat. "You don't need to do this."

"I don't need to do a great many things, Aksel. But this I want to do."

"I can help you."

"Don't beg, cupid. It's pathetic."

"You don't even want to know why we were pursuing you?"

I sighed. "Is this another pathetic attempt to save your life, or are you actually going to tell me?"

"Let me go and I'll tell you."

"Hard pass."

I held him out further.

"Okay!" he said quickly. "Okay! We wanted the child."

I frowned. "My child?" I asked and he nodded. "Why?"

"Heaven wanted your child," he amended.

"As in…God?"

Aksel shook his head as well as he was able with my hand around his neck. "No. No. The order came from Samael."

"That arsehat?" I muttered. "Why?"

"He didn't say."

I cocked my head. "No?"

"No."

"Then I guess you've served your usefulness."

I threw him into the pit. There was a torrent of fire and air, then all was still again. Still, expect for the slow clap from behind me.

I turned to see Cadriel applauding me. Drake stood next to him, his mouth open like he couldn't believe what he's just witnessed.

"Celestial looks good on you, Mrs Morningstar," Cadriel said appreciatively.

I went to take a little bow when I felt it.

Contraction.

My hand went to my stomach and I breathed out heavily.

"What's wrong?" Drake asked, already at my side.

"I think the baby's coming," I told him.

His face drained of colour, but he snapped at Cadriel to give him a hand getting me home.

I didn't even care that we flew because I was too busy counting.

Drake

"Get Isis!" Dad cried, running around the room. "Sinivali! Frigg! Juno! Hutellurra. Irsirra. Tawara. One of them have to be free. Brigid! Xochiquetzal. Everyone. GET EVERYONE!"

I slapped him across the cheek and he took a deep breath. As he turned back to face me, he smoothed his hair back again.

"Yes. Right. Good. Thank you, son."

"Calm the fuck down," I said to him. "If you lose your shit, I'm going to lose my shit. And I cannot afford to lose my shit."

Dad gave me a sympathetic smile. "Your wife's a fighter, Drake. She's my daughter-in-law. She won't give up."

I cleared my throat awkwardly and nodded. "No. 'Course she won't."

Wren had gone into labour. And if there was a time to freak out and wonder if I was ready to do this parenting thing, labour was the perfect time to do it. Right?

"Isn't there an Egyptian goddess you can call?" Wren called and I could hear the sass in her voice even as she breathed through another contraction.

"I did say 'Isis', did I not?" Dad muttered, looking around. I nodded.

"Funny story," Dad said, continuing on in lieu of silence. "We sort of absorbed them all. The Egyptians. There was a job for everyone – pretty much – when the Greeks came to power. So, we're all sort of already here."

"Who were you then?" she grunted.

"Oh. Um. Sort of Osiris. Little bit of Anubis. Everyone kind of had their finger in the dead and underworld pies back then. Very big into death, the Egyptians. Mortal death. Big on immortality. Role changed a little over time."

"That would make Grandad Ra," I said.

Dad nodded. "Of course, it did."

"Was he as big a fan of thunder back then as well?"

"He was still the god of the sky. Always with the sky, that one," Lucifer grumbled.

"Some could say always with the underworld with you," I pointed out.

"Look, is it my bad that I…don't like to be bossed around and end up here?" Dad asked with a shrug. "I'm never the all-powerful. It's always the guy with the sky."

"Once this is done, I'll make a new religion where they worship the shit out of the underworld," Wren groaned and squeezed the ever-living Heaven out of my hand as another contraction wracked her body.

At this rate, I was a touch concerned the baby was going to shred her to tiny pieces after all.

"I am fine," she grunted, glaring at me.

I swallowed and nodded. "Sure you are."

"The only part of my body that's not getting through this unscathed is my vagina, and I am assured that that's holy normal!"

I nodded again. "I have also heard that…"

"Here, ma'am. Ice chip?" Truman asked as he held the cup out to her.

She nodded and he popped one into her mouth. Wren breathed heavily through her nose and lay her head back for a moment.

Kyle clambered up on the end of the bed with a baseball glove on.

"What is that for?" Dad asked.

"To catch." He held it up like he was ready for anything.

"Kyle," Wren gritted out. "It's not a slide. You won't need to catch it."

Kyle seemed to deflate a little.

"But thank you for being ready to help."

"How help?" Kyle looked around at everyone.

The mandagot nudged his elbow gently as though in solidarity.

"Tell you what," Dad said. "How about–"

"Ugh. Like you know anything about childbirth," Persephone said as she strolled in the door.

"I know…" Dad paused. "All right, you've got me there. But what use are you?"

"Just because I never bore your children doesn't mean I didn't bear children, Hades," she fumed.

Dad's flames got a hint of the old blue about them. "Yes. Brilliant time to bring up your little indiscretions."

"My indiscretions?" Persephone cried. "What about yours?" She pointed at me. "There's the product of one right there. No offence, Drake darling."

I shook my head, not wanting to get in between these two. "All good."

"Not. All. Good," Wren said, trying to sit up.

And there was my wife, no longer mortal but facing down Lucifer and Persephone like she could incinerate them both with less than a thought.

"Very not all good. I am very soon going to be pushing a watermelon out of my vagina and I've got two holy gods arguing in the room. You want to argue?" Wren asked. "Then get out!"

Dad and Persephone were pushed towards the door. Wren's eyes were glowing a green to be almost yellow.

"I was just–" Dad started.

"I will not say it again," she warned them.

"Well," Dad said with a nod. "You are certainly not the goddess of tranquillity as your name would suggest."

"Lucifer!"

"Right. Yes. Sorry."

There was a flurry of activity. The most useful of which seemed to be conducted by Truman as he directed Ignacio and Kyle to get towels and more ice and whatever else Truman thought – knew? – he needed for birthing a baby.

Persephone took over holding Wren's hand for a while, while I stood around with my hands on my head and tried to breathe deeply enough to stave of the nausea.

Dad stood with me and was, for once, not even entertaining the notion of a song or dance.

"Ignacio, go and get Mr and Mrs Shaw, please," Truman said.

"What can I do?" I asked.

Truman gave me one look up and down. "Keep trying not to throw up, sir."

I nodded. "I can probably do that." I hoped.

I didn't even complain when Dad rubbed my back like I was a five year old who wouldn't sleep. It helped. It was calming. And I told myself that whatever kept me from freaking out was going to help Wren.

Wren, who was doing a million times better than I was.

She looked as uncomfortable as Heaven, but she wasn't complaining. Much. She certainly wasn't freaking out like I was.

It took a couple more hours before we got to the next stage. That involved a lot of yelling. Most of it was unintelligible, but I was pretty sure there was a lot of mentions about the importance of teaching kids about the consequences of sex whether you were mortal, celestial or something in between. Not that it was quite as succinct as that, but that was the gist.

There was also the breather where she apologised for yelling at me and said she didn't regret anything, she just hadn't been quite so ready for it to hurt that bad.

I shook my head. "You can call me any curse word under creation if it helps," I told her.

She reached for my hand and I took it gladly. Until another contraction hit and I was almost missing the days my wife was mortal and wouldn't have been able to hurt me if she tried.

"Okay," Truman said. "Time to push, ma'am."

20

Wren

"Mazel tov," Truman finally said. "It's a boy."

I had a new appreciation for mortal parents, but for mortal parents of Nephilim in particular.

Birthing one of those super strong, celestial bastards was something else. Even as an apparent celestial now myself, I didn't envy the mortal women who birthed Nephilim.

The birth itself passed by in a blur of pain and elation and yelling. I seemed to remember a lot of yelling, and most of it not very complimentary. It made me glad my parents hadn't made it to Hell in time to witness it.

There were enough witnesses as it was.

When I finally had my son in my arms, I almost forgot everything I'd just been through. Almost. For about ten seconds.

When he wrinkled his little nose and scrunched his little pink hands to his face, I was about ready to go for kid number two. Almost.

"He's gorgeous," Lucifer cooed, peering over Drake's shoulder.

I nodded. "He is."

"He's so tiny," Drake breathed as though he was afraid he'd hurt the baby just by talking or breathing too loudly.

"Have you talked about names yet?" Persephone asked.

"Shaw," Drake said proudly.

"A most excellent name."

We all looked over to see God standing in the room with a toy bunny.

"What are you doing here?" Lucifer huffed.

"I'm coming to see my great-grandson," he answered. "I brought a mortal present for him and I have a celestial present to give him as well."

"A celest..." Lucifer started. "Oh no! You're not giving him...?"

God nodded. "Why shouldn't I?"

"Does my grandson really need one of those filthy little things?" Lucifer asked, crossing his arms.

God turned a very paternal look on him. "He is my great-grandson and I will bestow a fitting gift upon him."

"You didn't seem to care about giving Drake any gifts."

"Drake wasn't born in our world."

"I thought you ruled over *all* of creation. Does that not mean that it's all your world?"

"You know what I meant. He was not born in a place I can more easily move about it."

"Yes," Lucifer huffed, "because Earth doesn't have a whole look for whatever this is. Silver fox they'd call you. They'd notice you all right, but they'd certainly not think you were their Lord and creator."

"Are you always this ungrateful when someone comes baring gifts?"

Before Lucifer could retort, I said quickly, "Thank you! That's very nice of you. I know Shaw will appreciate it."

"Yes," Lucifer sighed. "But a cherub in Hell? What will my subjects say?"

"They will no doubt have a wonderful time trying to kill him or at the very least annoy him."

Lucifer sighed heavily. "Well, its not like I can stop *you*, is it?"

God grinned and snapped his fingers. A chubby little baby-looking thing with little white wings appeared. It wore a leaf like a loin cloth and had a tuft of brown hair at the front of its head. It was about the same height as the devilbums, but had an aura of peace about it.

"My lord," it said with a little bow.

"Jeff, wonderful to see you."

"Jeff?" Lucifer asked, flabbergasted. "His name is Jeff?"

God nodded. "What do you expect him to be called?"

"Oh, I don't know. Something with an 'ael' or an 'iel' maybe. Daniel at the very least."

"My brother's name is Daniel, sir," Jeff said with an inclination of his little head.

Lucifer rolled his eyes. "Of course, he is. Fine. But if you get to bestow a gift upon Shaw, so do I."

I hated to think what he might come up with. Perhaps Cerberus had puppies hiding away somewhere. I could just picture our house and what state it would be in if we had a cerberus running around after Shaw in it. Not that it was terribly baby-proof just then either what with Ignacio's shark and weapons, Kyle's mandagot, and the general nature of Hell as a home for a small being.

Lucifer clicked his fingers and a devilbum appeared. It was facing away from us and bending over. Just as it fully appeared, it let out a huge fart. Shaw wriggled and I could have sworn he smiled.

I didn't know what the devilbum was waiting for, but he turned around slowly and confusion furrowed his forehead.

"Hi, boss," he said, looking around the room.

"Archie," Lucifer said with a wide smile to the room like everything was definitely going to plan. "I have a job for you."

Archie snapped his hooves together and saluted. "Ready, boss."

"I hereby officially give you as guardian to my grandson, Shaw Morningstar. It's your job–"

God cleared his throat and Lucifer shot him a sideways glare.

"It is your job – with Jeff the cherub – to protect Shaw, look after him, and help him learn the ways of his heritage."

"Aye, aye, your devilness!" Archie said. "It will be my honour." He gave Lucifer a wink.

Shaw cooed and both Jeff and Archie trotted over to see him. They eyed each other off carefully and, even though I was pretty new to this Heaven versus Hell thing, I understood that they were natural opposites if not natural enemies.

And they were apparently my son's new guardians.

This was going to be interesting.

Drake

From the moment he was born, Shaw had the whole of Hell and his great-grandad wrapped around his tiny littlest finger.

And it seemed he might have more magic in that little finger than I probably had in my whole body. Within hours of his birth, his green eyes were glowing a red to rival mine and I recognised the little wriggle he did with his shoulders; he was going to have wings that undoubtedly made an appearance at the least opportune time.

Wren's family came down to visit as soon as they could make it and they were as enamoured with Shaw as we already were. Once the families had said their hellos to Shaw, Truman and the boys ushered everyone down stairs and I brought Shaw when I followed them so Wren could get some sleep.

I lay Shaw in his bassinet and Kyle insisted that Kitty play guard along with Jeff and Archie.

While the others all talked and Truman and Ignacio ferried drinks and food around to the excited family members, I'd managed to get a moment alone with my grandfather.

"Yes, Drake?" he asked.

"I didn't say anything."

He tapped the side of his head. "You didn't have to. Omnipotent, remember?"

I sighed. "I was just wondering if…"

"If you can introduce Shaw to your mother?"

"Yes."

He seemed to think about it for a moment. Finally, he nodded. "I cannot release her from heaven again, even on a day pass. But I will allow you to bring Shaw to meet her."

"And exactly how do I get him in there?" I asked, thinking there must be some kind of loophole situation; both of us were of Heaven after all. "And how will I get both of us back out again?"

Grandad smiled at me knowingly. "You are a clever one. However, I have no intention of trying to keep your son somewhere you do not wish him to be."

I was still trying to get used to the idea of 'my son', I almost missed him continue.

"As for how you will enter and exit. I do believe you have three very useful young beings who found themselves a back door and remembered to leave it propped open for next time."

I frowned. "The boys?"

Grandad nodded. "I may have…chosen to overlook the knowledge of how they got in. Not an easy task after the stink they caused. Michael has been quite beside himself since."

I honestly couldn't care less about Uncle Michael's state of mind. In fact, the more beside himself he was, the better I felt. I'd never met him, but I didn't need to meet him to know he was a bigger arsehole than Samael and Azazel put together.

"And when he finds the door?"

Grandad tapped his nose. "Your uncle won't find the door, Drake. So long as it is used with extreme discretion, I will allow its existence and position to remain as much a secret as I'm able to keep it."

"Discretion? So, the visit doesn't have to be a one-time thing?" I asked, trying not to let myself hope.

Grandad put his hands in his pockets and shrugged wily. "What I don't know, won't hurt anyone."

"But you're omnipotent."

"I'm also very old. Perhaps my memory isn't what it used to be."

"Ugh," I heard my father say and turned to see him watching us. "Enough with the good guy routine. We get it, you're awesome."

I'm not sure I would have gone so far as to say my grandfather was awesome, but I was starting to think he wasn't quite such a colossal git as I'd thought he was.

"And if the cupids discover Shaw's in Heaven and try to keep him there?" I asked.

"I will personally make sure that no one keeps your son anywhere you or he doesn't want him to be." He paused and seemed to catch Dad's eye.

"What is it?" Dad asked.

"Huh. Must be Shaw."

"What must?"

"The prophecy."

"What prophecy?"

Grandad was obviously trying to hide his exasperation. "You know. The big one. *The* one."

"The apocalypse?"

"That one."

"You think Shaw's the one foretold to raise Hell on Earth?"

"Or Heaven." Grandad nodded.

"True."

"But yes. He's certainly got the power for it."

"Well, damn."

The bells of Hell tolled out ominously, thundering through my very bones.

"They certainly seem to think so," Grandad said.

"That would make sense why your goons were trying to woo my daughter-in-law to the dark side," Dad said petulantly. "They wanted Shaw for themselves."

"I had nothing to do with that."

"You never do," Dad muttered. "How is it that a bunch of try-hards worked it out before we did?"

Grandad looked at the little sleeping bundle in his bassinet. He gently lay his fingers on Shaw's belly. Shaw's face scrunched in his sleep, then his lips curved like he was smiling.

"Prophecies have a nasty habit of being self-fulfilling. The fact that Samael was concerned enough to try to turn Wren before Shaw was born and that we have now voiced our question out loud, we may well have ensured the little one's fate."

"Shaw will be his own man," I said vehemently.

"We each of us have a destiny, son. Often we think we are escaping it only to realise we are guaranteeing it."

As the clanging of the bells of Hell faded away once more, I looked at my son. He fussed in his sleep and I picked him up, careful not to wake him.

I'd thought nothing could scare me now. I'd thought the idea of an impending baby was terrifying. I'd thought a part of me wanted a normal life – by human standards, at least.

Holding Shaw in my arms, I was starkly reminded to be careful what I wished for. After all, what was more normal or scary than being responsible for an actual baby?

...your favourite characters and more will be back again soon. There are many more stories planned in the Heaven and Hell Chronicles.

Damned if I know

You can check out the playlist for this series on Spotify. Just click or scan the QR code.

Thank you so much for reading this story! Word of mouth is super valuable to authors. So, if you have a few moments to rate/review Wren and Drake's story – or, even just pass it on to a friend – I would be really appreciative.

Have you looked for my books in store, or at your local or school library and can't find them? Just let your friendly staff member or librarian know that they can order copies directly from LightningSource/Ingram.

If you want to keep up to date with my new releases, rambles and writing progress, sign up to my newsletter at https://landing.mailerlite.com/webforms/landing/y1n6q2.

Follow me:

Thanks

I'd like to say a big thank you to personal things for getting in the way of finishing this book on time. I was going to do amazing things and be amazing, and you just had to come and rain on my parade.

To Charny, as usual, for reading it and cheering me on. I honestly don't know what I'd do without your instantaneous feedback – you spoil me.

Thanks to my husband for keeping me fed and watered while I did the big last final push to get this all finished. As promised, it's the last set deadline for a while.

And a final thank you to my previous obsession with collecting mythology books for helping me when Google couldn't.

My Books

Scarlett's list is just starting out, but you can find where to buy all my books in print and eBook at my website; www.elizabethstevens.com.au/.

About the Author

Scarlett Knox is the Paranormal Darker/Bully Romance penname of bestselling author Elizabeth Stevens. Scarlett is the name to read if you want darker/bully romance in the Mature YA/NA crossover space with paranormal elements. Think high school, college, and academy. Add in superpowers, vampires and werewolves, angels and demons, and more. Scarlett brings my usual wit, banter, and repartee in good old enemies-to-lovers showdowns between alpha males and the sassy heroines strong enough to kick them to their knees.

Writer. Reader. Perpetual student. Nerd.

Born in New Zealand to a Brit and an Australian, I am a writer with a passion for all things storytelling. I love reading, writing, TV and movies, gaming, and spending time with family and friends. I am an avid fan of British comedy, superheroes, and SuperWhoLock. I have too many favourite books, but I fell in love with reading after Isobelle Carmody's *Obernewtyn*. I am obsessed with all things mythological – my current focus being old-style Irish faeries. I live in Adelaide (South Australia) with my long-suffering husband, delirious dog, mad cat, two chickens, and a lazy turtle.

<u>Contact me:</u>

Email: scarlettknox@elizabethstevens.com.au
Website: www.elizabethstevens.com.au/scarlet-knox
Twitter: www.twitter.com/writer_iz
Instagram: www.instagram.com/writeriz
Facebook: https://www.facebook.com/elizabethstevens88/

9 781925 928259